Aw
BOTANIC HILL DETECTIVES MYSTERIES

BOOK 1—NUTMEG STREET: EGYPTIAN SECRETS

Mom's Choice Book Awards:
Gold Award for Juvenile Fiction—General

Moonbeam Children's Book Awards:
Gold Award for Pre-Teen Fiction: Mystery

American Book Fest Awards:
2020 Best Book Award for Children's Fiction

Royal Dragonfly Book Awards:
Second Place (tie) in Historical Fiction
Second Place in Mystery

The Wishing Shelf Book Awards:
2020 Finalist

Kops-Fetherling International Book Awards:
Phoenix Award for Best New Voice—Fiction, Middle Grade, Ages 8-12

Independent Publisher Book Awards:
2021 Gold Award for Best First Book, Juvenile/Young Adult

International Book Awards:
2021 Finalist, Best New Fiction

Independent Audiobook Awards:
Finalist, Young Adult for Tom Jordan, Narrator

American Fiction Awards:
2021 Winner, Pre-Teen Fiction

AWARDS FOR THE
BOTANIC HILL DETECTIVES MYSTERIES

(continued)

BOOK 2—EUCALYPTUS STREET: GREEN CURSE

Mom's Choice Book Awards:
Gold Award for Juvenile Fiction—General

Moonbeam Children's Book Awards:
Gold Award for Pre-Teen Fiction: Mystery

Story Monsters Approved:
2020 Winner, First Place in Tween Novels Fiction
First Place in Making a Difference
Third Place in Middle Grade Fiction, Ages 8-12

San Diego Book Awards:
2021 Winner
Finalist in Children's Fiction

Purple Dragonfly Awards:
2021 Winner
Honorable Mention in Charity/Making a Difference
Winner, Honorable Mention in Mystery

A BOTANIC HILL DETECTIVES MYSTERY | BOOK 3

WALNUT STREET:

PHANTOM RIDER

BY

SHERRILL JOSEPH

ACORN PUBLISHING

FROM THE TINY ACORN...
GROWS THE MIGHTY OAK

Walnut Street: Phantom Rider. First Edition
Copyright © 2021 Sherrill M. Joseph. All rights reserved.
Printed in the United States of America. For information, address
Acorn Publishing, LLC, 3943 Irvine Blvd. Ste. 218, Irvine, CA 92602

www.acornpublishingllc.com
Cover design by eBook Launch

Digital Formatting and Interior Design by Debra Cranfield Kennedy

Library of Congress Control Number: 2021910935

ISBN: 978-1-952112-70-6

Dedicated to all the horsewomen who have
Trotted, cantered, or galloped into my life:

Barb Rasmussen—forever friend and yoga cowgirl

Janet Horne—first cousin and first-rate horse breeder

Laura Galecki—riding instructor extraordinaire

Mary Asher-Fitzpatrick—friend since childhood
and serious equestrienne

"N. J."—world's best daughter
and former horseback rider

And

Black Cowboys and Black Cowgirls,

Past and present, forgotten and remembered

"As a kid, I didn't see Black cowboys on the screen.
What that said to me was that there were things
I couldn't do or be because of my color.
What we see others like us do gives us
permission to expand our own horizons."

WALTER DEAN MYERS (1937-2014),
AMERICAN AUTHOR OF MONSTER,
BAD BOY: A MEMOIR, ET AL.

CONTENTS

WALNUT STREET:

PHANTOM RIDER

BASS REEVES,
DEPUTY UNITED STATES MARSHAL

*Bass Reeves is the real-life model
for our fictional character,
Deputy United States Marshal Aloysius "Papa" Mayfield.*

Bass Reeves was born into slavery in Crawford County, Arkansas, in July 1838. His owner was a landowner and state legislator named Reeves. It was not uncommon for Black slaves to be given an owner's last name.

Later, the entire household moved to Texas. The boy slave grew up not knowing how to read or write and remained illiterate his entire life.

Bass escaped from his owner during the Civil War and fled to the Indian Territory, later called Oklahoma. There, he hid out, living among at least five different tribes of Indians, who trusted him more than they did White men. He learned their languages fluently and their customs, how to track and ride horses, and shoot guns expertly.

After slavery was abolished in 1865, Bass Reeves returned to Arkansas as a free man. There, he bought a farm, married, and had eleven children.

In 1875, because he knew the Indians' ways and had good detective skills, he was offered the deputy United States marshal job to return to Oklahoma to bring back, dead or alive, the many outlaws hiding there. This made Bass Reeves the first deputy United States marshal of African descent west of the Mississippi River.

Deputy U.S. Marshal Reeves was a polite man with

broad shoulders, tall at six feet, two inches, especially atop his white horse. He was a sharp dresser, though he often wore disguises to catch horse thieves, bootleggers, rustlers, and murderers. He never brought in the wrong man, despite not knowing how to read a wanted poster.

When Reeves retired in 1907, he had arrested and delivered over 3,000 felons—including one of his own sons. He received fame and substantial reward money for his efforts. The deputy shot and killed fourteen outlaws in self-defense, though he preferred not to kill. Reeves himself was never shot, but his tall hat sustained some bullet holes. He also survived many assassination attempts, including a close call when his coat button was shot off.

Reeves's longevity as a lawman is a remarkable testament to his skills since more than 250 marshals, deputy marshals, and special deputy marshals have been killed in the line of duty in the United States since the position was established by the Judiciary Act of 1789 and signed into law by President George Washington.

Bass Reeves died of natural causes at the age of seventy-two on January 12, 1910, in Muskogee, Oklahoma. He was buried there, but the exact location of his grave is unknown.

He remains a legend to this day.

When you finish reading *Walnut Street: Phantom Rider*, please return to this page. Compare and contrast Bass Reeves and Papa Mayfield.

Sources: *Wikipedia, Britannica.com, BlackPast.org, truewestmagazine.com, and usmarshals.gov.*

CHAPTER ONE

· ✧ ·

A Mystery from Walnut Street

Moki Kalani couldn't stop thinking about three things that warm October afternoon in Southern California. First, his pineapple-coconut upside-down cake, which he had baked for the Mayfields' potluck barbecue on Walnut Street, was a hit. The guests had gobbled up almost every crumb, and the empty dessert plate in his hand provided the final proof. Second, the four amateur detectives—the twins Lanny and Lexi Wyatt, Rani Kumar, and Moki himself—tended to learn of their next mystery case as a squad. This time, the thirteen-year-old Hawaiian boy had a heads up that required his pledge of secrecy. Third, the secret's details could finally be revealed once the barbecue ended.

Moki's newest friend, thirteen-year-old Ben Mayfield, had provided the heads up. The two boys had been playing tennis at a nearby park when Moki sensed something besides sports on Ben's mind. He had a problem that needed telling, and Moki was a willing listener. Moki had moved to California from Honolulu, Hawai'i, five years ago. He and Ben had become friends recently. They shared a love of tennis, horseback riding, and surfing. Most important, they already trusted one another.

The barbecue was Ben's, and he'd convinced his parents to invite the entire detective squad—then hire them to solve an ongoing, annoying problem at the Mayfields' horse ranch and youth saddle club about two hours east of town. Ben's parents had confidence in their son and in Moki, so they had agreed to the plan. But now, Ben had his own private reason far beyond his parents' motivation for wanting the detectives' help. Last month, he alone had witnessed a terrifying spectacle at the ranch. He hadn't shared it yet with his family—or with Moki.

Ben walked into the dining room through the patio doors of the family's spacious Victorian house. In a few strides, he was next to Moki, who set his dessert plate and plastic fork down on a nearby table. Most of the partygoers had thanked their hosts and said their good-byes. Only the other three detectives, Mr. and Mrs. Mayfield, and four guests remained on the now much quieter patio.

"Hey, Moki," said Ben as he chucked his friend on his tanned arm. "Sorry I made you keep your new case a secret. Hope it hasn't been a problem. My parents wanted to check off this monthly barbecue before dealing with our ranch situation. I probably shouldn't have said anything."

Moki returned the friendly jab to Ben's brown arm.

"It's okay, dude. You needed to share your family's problem. I respect that. It was kind of hard, though. We detectives are a tight group that always shares everything." Moki hung his head, and his thick black hair fell over his eyes. "I didn't give them any details, but I did kind of hint that I had some information."

Indeed, Moki had let slip at the conclusion of the squad's last case that a new mystery was already brewing. He didn't mention that it was on Walnut Street. His friends had been hounding him ever since. Finally, they would get the specifics.

Seeing Moki and Ben talking, the other detectives entered the dining room. Lanny, the head of the detective agency, was in the lead.

"Okay, Moki, spill," Lanny said. "Oh, wait—" he turned to Ben. "Excuse me, Ben. Great party." He turned back to Moki. "*Now* spill."

Lexi and Rani set down their drinks and moved closer, at full listening attention. The detectives were more than ready for their new case.

One year ago, they'd created the Botanic Hill Detectives Agency, naming it after the beautiful neighborhood in which they all lived in sun-soaked Las Palmitas, a California resort town on the Pacific coast. The agency had earned local and international fame for its success in solving mysteries and crimes that baffled law enforcement officials. Just a couple weeks before, the squad had wrapped up their second case, *Eucalyptus Street: Green Curse*. They had spent many days and nights in a spooky nearby mansion, hunting for a multimillion-dollar cursed emerald. As always, once a mystery was solved, they longed for their next adventure. The Mayfields knew all about the agency's reputation, and now a tantalizing new case was about to unfold on Walnut Street.

Lexi stood with her hands on her hips, a longer-haired brunette version of her dark blond twin brother. Rani next to her wore a thoughtful expression, her intense brown eyes matching the brown threads in the peacock pattern on her handmade sari. Rani's grandmother, who had come with then five-year-old Rani and her parents when they'd moved from India to California, still lovingly made the saris Rani wore nearly every day.

Before Moki or Ben could respond, a crash and breaking glass sounded from the patio. The five teens raced to the scene. An eleven-year-old girl named Catherine Sims had just shoved twelve-year-old Lionel James against the punch bowl table. The bowl now lay in glittering shards on the cement floor. The sticky red drink leftovers had splashed everywhere.

"Now, what's happened here?" Mrs. Mayfield asked calmly but with authority. She was strong, as evidenced by her toned biceps, but took a gentle hold of each child's arm to look them over and to keep them separated. "Are you two all right?" Mrs. Mayfield used to be a school counselor. She now used her training to visit local schools and scout for "at-risk" students with behavioral or emotional issues who would be good candidates for the Mayfields' horse therapy saddle club at their ranch east of town.

"Lionel said all girls are weaklings," Catherine explained. "I was showing him how wrong he was." She looped her thick copper braids behind her ears. The scowl on her freckled face promised more trouble between the two. "And I won't go to the ranch if he'll be there."

"Girls are still weaklings, even if you did push me down," Lionel replied. "You caught me off guard, that's all." Lionel's dark narrowed eyes signaled his plan to get even.

"Next time, Catherine, challenge a boy to an arm-wrestling match instead—with an adult referee," Mrs. Mayfield said. "Maybe my punch bowl would still be intact if you had. Otherwise, keep your hands to yourself. And Lionel, remember how we talked about processing through the term 'T.H.I.N.K.' before you speak? Ask yourself if what you're about to say or do is *True, Helpful, Inspiring, Necessary,* and *Kind.* If you can truthfully answer yes to all five, then speak your mind. If not, don't even go there. The world has enough violence and hate. Counteract those with kindness. Got it?" She slowly let go of each child's arm as she felt them relax.

"For goodness sakes, Lionel Deshaun James!" his mother interrupted. "You apologize to Mrs. Mayfield and Catherine right this instant."

After a brief pause, he said, "Aww, okay . . . sorry." He kicked the ground with his foot and made no eye contact with anyone. But then, he looked up. "Catherine better apologize, too."

"Yes. You, too, Catherine Renee," her own mother said.

"And you're going to pay for that punch bowl out of your allowance. When will you learn to control your temper?"

Catherine stared at the ground and whispered, "Sorry, Mrs. Mayfield. Sorry, Lionel."

"I accept your apologies," Mrs. Mayfield replied. "But what's more important, do you accept the other's apology?"

The two nodded, staring at the floor.

Mrs. Mayfield continued. "Apparently, I need to repeat to you two kids what's expected of you as guests at the ranch. Ms. James? Ms. Sims? Will you also come out to the front porch with us, please?" Mrs. Mayfield moved to the door.

The Mayfields had held the barbecue to welcome Catherine and Lionel as the newest members of their ranch's saddle club. Ben was always in charge of the details. Former club kids had also attended the Walnut Street party that afternoon to share their experiences. All had gone smoothly until the punch bowl incident.

"Oh, and dear," Mrs. Mayfield said, turning to her husband. "Will you see to Gracie, Ben, and his friends, and get that discussion underway? I'll join you as soon as I can."

"Will do, Edie," tall, muscular Ezra Mayfield replied. "But first, Catherine and Lionel, look right here at me." He pointed to his eyes. "Now, you listen to Mrs. Mayfield. We have strict rules at the ranch and saddle club. You need to follow them to keep yourselves and others safe. Understand?"

"Yes, Mr. Mayfield," the two said in unison as they shuffled out with downcast eyes.

Gracie was Ben's skinny kid sister. He loved his sibling, whose hair was a pouf of springy ebony coils that bounced with her every movement. But he wasn't too happy to have a ten-year-old mixing with his friends. More important, Ben wanted to shield Gracie as well as his parents from that scary scene at the ranch until he and the detectives could make sense of it. Despite that, he knew that ranch problems, big and small, tended to be family business, and his sister was family. So this time, even with what Ben felt was a genuine new danger at their ranch, there could be no excluding her. The boy had decided that, this afternoon, he would some-how reveal his nightmarish secret to his four friends—but in private. He would have to find a way.

For her part, Gracie was thrilled to be around the famous detectives. She had taken an instant liking to Lexi and Rani. At the barbecue, the two girls had told Gracie about the henna tattoos that covered their hands and arms. Rani promised to paint some on Gracie sometime.

Beyond tattoos, the young girl had been secretly dreaming for ages to help the four teens solve a mystery. With her parents about to present the squad with a new case, she felt certain her chance to be a junior detective had arrived.

CHAPTER TWO

· ✧ ·

A Golden Mystery

With Saturday's Saddle Club Welcome Barbecue officially ended, Mr. Mayfield led his group into the study to acquaint them with some mysterious occurrences out at their ranch. Mrs. Mayfield would join them once she had spoken privately with the newest saddle club kids and their mothers.

In the study, little Gracie plopped onto a long brown leather couch covered with hopsack pillows that had cacti and armadillos stitched on them. The detectives grouped around a large photo on the wall.

"Ben, is that a *paniolo* in the picture?" Moki asked. The man in the photo was a tall, muscle-bound Black man in full cowboy dress wearing a large brass star on his vest. It was an old photo, a bit out of focus. He looked like a sheriff from the Old West. The photo's rustic wooden frame fit the image.

Seeing the puzzled look on his friend's face, Moki

translated. "Oh sorry, dude. *Paniolo* is Hawaiian for 'cowboy.'"

"Yeah, that's my five-time great-grandfather, Aloysius Mayfield. He was a famous Black cowboy. In fact, he was an important Black deputy U.S. marshal for California in the 1860s—one of the first in our state. Deputy Marshal Mayfield. Friends just called him Papa, though."

"Cool," Lexi said, her green eyes flashing. "How come I never heard of Papa Mayfield? . . . Oh, wait, I know why. Unfortunately, too many African Americans have been left out of history books because of racism and discrimination."

"That's tragic but true," Ben replied. Then, glancing up from the rug, he continued with more emphasis, "Black cowboys and Black cowgirls have definitely been left out of history books. And most movies have only White cowboys. I figure lots of people still think all Old West cowboys were White. Did you know that one in four cowboys back then was Black?"

"Wow. I do now," Rani said. "And I think everyone needs to know that."

"Ben, what are the chances Papa has something to do with the ranch mystery?" Lanny asked. Hope was evident on his face. Cowboys, ranches, and mysteries, all in one lump? Could they be that lucky?

"I strongly suspect so," Mr. Mayfield answered instead. He was already seated in his overstuffed, brown leather easy chair. "You see, Papa was the original owner and builder of our ranch east of here in the mountains near the old historic town of Cody. He named it Gold Mine Acres Ranch."

"A gold mine is involved, too?" Lanny said. "Best case ever!"

He and Moki high-fived.

Ben's dad laughed. "Well, I'm a bit less thrilled about it."

Lexi elbowed her brother. Rani did the same to Moki.

"The case involves a gold mine, Mr. Mayfield?" Lexi asked more professionally.

"It does. One of Papa's jobs as a deputy marshal was to bring order to lawlessness that often ruled the gold mining camps of California. He captured outlaws but also became interested in mining for gold himself. Over the years, he made a sizable fortune collecting rewards for fugitives he arrested and brought in. When he retired from his deputy marshal duties, he moved down here from Northern California. Gold had been found in Cody, so Papa bought some land on the outskirts of that town, built Gold Mine Acres Ranch there, and established a base camp for gold mining."

"And . . . he struck *gold*!" Gracie shouted, throwing both arms up to the ceiling.

"That he did, Gracie." Her dad leaned back in his chair. "He found a rich gold vein in a mine on his property."

Ben added, "Many legends are still told by Cody's residents about Papa as a lawman and a gold miner, and about his mine and property. Papa kept the mine's location a secret, except not from his partners, of course. Many people tried to get them to tell, but they never did—as far as we know."

"And now you think someone is looking for it," Rani said with a faraway gaze.

Ben's dad replied, "That seems to me to be a logical assumption—" He was about to explain when he noticed his wife standing at the study door.

"Dear, before you tell our detective guests another word," she said, "I think it's time for Gracie to come with me to help clean up from the barbecue." She beckoned to her wide-eyed daughter with a curl of her pointer finger and eyes that meant business.

"Aw, Mom," Gracie said. She scowled and grabbed a large sofa pillow, clutching it to her chest. "I want to stay. It was just getting good. And why doesn't Ben have to come help, too?"

"Do as your mother says, Gracie darlin'. Ben will be doing his share later," Mr. Mayfield replied. He pursed his lips, raised his eyebrows, and pointed to the study door.

Gracie rose to leave, her rebellion clear as she still clutched the pillow and walked in slow motion with a scowl. Rani caught the little girl's eye, then nodded her head slightly, winking at her. Gracie winked back shyly, smiled, gently tossed the pillow onto the sofa, and skipped from the room. Her fluffy hair bounced with her.

Mr. Mayfield stood up and closed the study door behind his daughter. In a few strides, he was back in his favorite chair. "Ben, I do expect you to help them later."

In his excitement, Lanny didn't wait for Ben to respond to his father's comment. He asked, "Mr. Mayfield, do you happen to know where the gold mine is?"

"No, I don't. We don't even know if it still exists. There don't seem to be any records of it at the ranch or in Cody. But someone seems to want to find it and is losing patience."

"What exactly has happened to convince you of that?" Lexi asked.

"Well, ranch items are disappearing at an increasingly alarming rate. My theory is someone is trying to harass us into selling our property. If a gold mine does exist there, that someone might think they'd make a bundle off the ranch if we were gone, so they could find gold. That would increase the value of our property, too. Greed is a powerful motivator."

Ben said, "And we've noticed other stuff happening."

"Like what?" Moki asked.

"Unidentified horse tracks," Ben said, "and unidentified human footprints all over the property, near the house, barn, corrals, and guest bunkhouse. As for the things that've gone missing—they're random. It doesn't make sense." He had slid off the sofa and onto the rug, hugging his knees.

Moki joined his friend on the floor, tucked up his knees to match Ben's, and listened. "Maybe we can help you make some sense of it, dude. What have you noticed missing?"

"Little things at first," he said. "Like ropes, garden tools, and water buckets. They disappeared. But it's increased to horse bridles and blankets and some clothes drying on the line. About a month ago, a saddle club kid's entire suitcase was stolen, and the bunkhouse was, like, ransacked or something. Clothes and furniture were tossed all over the place. A total mess."

Mr. Mayfield added, "As the news traveled back to Las Palmitas, it negatively affected attendance at our saddle club. And that hurts kids we could be helping. We were lucky to convince Catherine's and Lionel's moms to let them visit. Some say Gold Mine Acres Ranch is haunted. Of course, that's completely ridiculous. But those rumors have proven difficult to quash with each new theft."

Lanny frowned and said, "That's terrible. Has anything else happened?"

"Yes," Mr. Mayfield replied. He strode across the room and pulled a paper out of his top desk drawer. "A few weeks ago, we found this note nailed to the tack room wall."

Like in a movie, the note had cut-out words and letters that read, "Get out or expect worse losses."

Rani fingered the cryptic message. "And the police haven't discovered who's behind this?"

Mr. Mayfield sighed and shrugged his shoulders. "Sheriff Buckley from Cody has been out to the ranch after each theft, but no luck yet."

"And FYI, there weren't any fingerprints on that note," Ben added with a frown.

Never one to be shy, Moki asked, "Do you think someone has any other motives besides finding the gold mine . . . like, could you be getting harassed because you're Black?"

"Thanks for asking, Moki," Ben's dad said. "That idea did cross my mind, but I don't feel these occurrences are racially motivated. There's nothing about this harassment that seems directed toward us personally. It's just ruining our business by scaring off potential saddle club kids. All of this leads me to believe someone wants to run us out, not because of who we are, but because of what we might leave behind."

"That could be a reasonable theory," Lanny replied. "What can we do to help?" He eyed his squad members, who nodded.

Mr. Mayfield was once again sitting on the edge of his chair. He leaned forward, fingertips pressed together. "We're hoping you kids can come out to the ranch for a week starting this coming Monday when Catherine and Lionel are there. Maybe you four can get to the bottom of these strange occurrences."

"We'd be happy to do that," Lanny said with his blue-violet eyes sparkling.

"That's wonderful," Mr. Mayfield replied. "I'll call each of your parents to discuss the details and get their permission. We'll see you Monday morning if all goes well. Any help you can offer will be greatly appreciated."

With that, he rose to leave the room. "Thanks again. I think that's all we know for right now. And Ben, don't forget to come help with clean-up as soon as your friends leave."

The kids thanked Mr. Mayfield, and he left the study.

Before the detectives could say a word, Ben put his finger to his lips and motioned for the squad to follow him. At last, his chance to share his burning secret with the detectives had come.

On tiptoe, he led all four kids up the back staircase to his room. Once there, he shut the door. Perspiration beaded his forehead. "There's more. I've seen something—or, to be more exact, someone—at the ranch."

The squad quickly encircled the nervous boy. "Who, dude?" Moki whispered.

"I call him the Phantom Rider."

CHAPTER THREE

· ◇ ·

The Phantom Rider

The Botanic Hill detectives were glad to finally know the details Moki had been keeping secret about the strange occurrences at the Mayfields' mountain ranch. Ben's additional revelation about a "Phantom Rider" certainly added more intrigue to their new mystery case.

"You said 'him' when referring to the Phantom Rider," Lanny replied as the group huddled in Ben's room. "How do you know it's a guy?"

"Because of the way he sat in the saddle. And because he's very tall and muscular."

"Details, dude, details," Moki added. "Give us the what, when, where, why, and how."

"Please start with where and when you saw him," Lexi said with her arms behind her back, resisting the urge to grab Ben's forearm. She had a bad habit of squeezing skin when she was anxious or trying to pry information out of someone. It especially drove Lanny crazy.

"Well, the first time was about a month ago when my family and I were at the ranch house for the most recent saddle club session. I was woken late one night by the sound of a horse approaching. My room is on the second floor facing north, overlooking the side yard with a view of the barn and bunkhouse. I looked out the open window to investigate. The moon was full, so I could see him clear as day right below me." Ben's whole body shivered.

Rani said, "Ben, I know you're nervous, but I need to ask. What exactly did you see? And why do you call him 'the Phantom Rider'?" She felt her own heart beating faster as Ben spoke.

"I saw a man on a skittish white Arabian stallion between the barn and the ranch house. The guy sat tall in the saddle, the reins held high, leading the horse to rear up. Like something out of a corny old Western movie. As I said, the moon was full and bright, but the man was almost invisible. That's why I call him a phantom."

"Invisible?" Rani blurted. "Can you explain what you mean?"

"Right. Please describe him," Lanny pressed. "What could you see? Was he dressed like an old movie cowboy, too?"

"He was wearing all black, head to toe. Would've blended into the darkness if it hadn't been for the moonlight. He wore what looked like a shiny black leather outfit, with black boots, big black gloves with flaring cuffs, and a black western hat. But the creepy part was he had on what I think was a black ski mask. His entire head and face were covered—except for his eyes and mouth."

"I get the feeling your parents don't know about this since you called us up here to your room to tell us in private," Moki said. "Did you tell Sheriff Buckley during one of his visits?"

"No way! I'm not going to tell the police and my parents that I saw some invisible phantom guy in the middle of the night. They'd think I was crazy," Ben said as he hugged himself and paced the floor. "You're the only ones I've told."

Lanny and Moki exchanged worried looks. The room went quiet for a few seconds.

Ben stopped pacing, turned to the others, and added, "Okay, okay. There's more. You know what's creepiest of all? He saw me." Ben hugged himself again. "The Phantom Rider saw me." His voice quavered. Then, more steadily, "I probably gasped or something when I saw him, because he looked up, right at me. Without a word, he shook his fist at me. I took that as a big-time threat not to say anything. Then, he rode away. Whoever he is, he's a good rider, too, the way he controlled the horse the whole time. Freaked me out. Still freaks me out thinking about him."

"Yeah, dude. That's scary stuff," Moki replied. "But you said 'the first time you saw him.' What about the next time?"

"I think I saw him one other time but at a distance. It was the next night at dusk. At least, I saw the white horse.

It's one fine animal. I'm assuming the Phantom was riding it. It—or they—were galloping away at the far edge of our ranch's property, heading northeast. And I mean fast."

"So, what's northeast of the ranch?" Lexi asked.

"Not much for miles. Just a desert town called Rainbow Flats. Well, it used to be a town. Now, it's a ghost town. You know, abandoned. No one goes there anymore. A film crew made a movie there a few years back and, supposedly, left a bunch of the props."

Rani frowned. "Any guesses as to who the Phantom Rider might be?"

"No, since most of the men in and near Cody are big, brawny, muscular guys like him, so it could be any of them."

"None of the saddle club kids heard anything, right?" asked Moki. "Any hired hands or other workers on the property who might have seen or heard the Phantom Rider that first night?"

"No one reported hearing or seeing anything. I think a kid would have screamed if they'd seen the Phantom. And we do have two hired hands at the ranch. Their quarters are off the far side of the barn and across from the bunkhouse. So they couldn't have seen the Phantom from where they were. I asked them the next day, anyway, by saying I had heard something the night before. They didn't report anything unusual. Makes me wonder if I've been seeing things."

"I doubt that, dude," Moki replied with a smile.

"Do you think the Phantom Rider is responsible for the thefts?" Lexi asked.

"Maybe, though the thefts started long before I saw the Phantom. Can't prove it."

"So, we don't know for certain what the Phantom Rider is doing or why, or who he is, or if he or someone else is stealing the ranch stuff," Lanny added. "But we're going to find out."

CHAPTER FOUR

· ✧ ·

Off to Gold Mine Acres Ranch

Two days after the squad had learned the mysterious details of their new case, the Mayfields' gigantic beige van pulled into the twins' circular driveway on Quince Street. It was nine o'clock on the dot. The Mayfields had already picked up Catherine and Lionel, who sat silently behind the two adults. Gracie was between both kids on the bench seat. There were still two more rows toward the back of the vehicle. Ben waved from one of them.

The four detectives waved back. All were anxious to begin their new case and spend a week at the ranch. Rani and Moki had arrived a half-hour earlier out of sheer excitement. The kids' pile of suitcases and gear was on the front porch of the twins' large house. The detectives' parents were there to see them off.

Mrs. Mayfield shook each parent's hand. "We're so grateful the detectives have agreed to come out to the country to help us."

"Thanks for having confidence in our fabulous four-some," Dr. Ian Wyatt, the twins' famous archaeologist dad, said with a smile.

Lexi had walked to the passenger door. She admired the company logo on the side of the van. It showed a golden horseshoe topping a circle of five different-colored hands with touching fingertips. These were superimposed on a horse's head. Around it were the words, "Gold Mine Acres Ranch and Youth Saddle Club. Cody, California."

Everyone helped Mr. Mayfield load the kids' belongings into the van's spacious back storage compartment. Suddenly, Moki looked concerned. "Lots of suitcases and gear, Ben. But where's the food?"

"Dude, it's already at the ranch." Ben playfully hit his forehead with the heel of his hand. "Don't you remember? I texted you yesterday that my great-aunt Maisie's out there. She's a super cook and has our menus planned for the whole week. And believe it or not, there is a grocery store in Cody. You aren't going to starve, dude."

"*I ka he kokua*—uh, translation, 'that's a relief.'" Moki wiped his brow dramatically.

"And you better not have brought any food along," Ben said to Moki. "It'll be taken away. It's not allowed in the bunkhouse, because it can attract bugs and animals."

Moki shivered. "I didn't. But holy hissers! I'd give up food any day to keep snakes out of my bed."

"Wait," Lexi said, holding both hands up as if to signal for silence. "Did I hear Moki the foodie say he'd 'give up food'? That's a first." Lexi and Rani high-fived. She was, of course, referring to the fact that Moki never missed a meal if he could help it.

"Snakes always change the plan," Moki replied. He was no fan of venomous reptiles.

Minutes later, good-byes and good wishes for a fun week were said, and the van was off.

A mile down the road, Ben was the first to speak. "I almost forgot. Did you guys remember to bring your Halloween costumes? We always have a farewell barn dance on Saturday before we go back home on Sunday, and this year, it lands smack on Halloween night. How cool is that?"

"Very!" Moki said.

"Costumes are packed," Lanny replied for all the detectives. Then his face lit up. He pulled down on Ben's shoulder and whispered in his ear, "But we're going to spend this coming week at the ranch making sure the Phantom Rider never gets to wear his again."

Ben beamed.

Rani turned around and handed some papers to Lanny. "This is some information from my dad to help us find Papa's gold mine. I picked his brain last night." Rani's dad was a professor of geology at Las Palmitas University and knew the area around Cody well.

"Wow! Thanks," Lanny said. He perused the sheets before putting them into a knapsack around his neck. The boy had done some research himself and had packed a gold test kit, which included a small magnet, a pocketknife, a piece of glass, and a bit of unglazed tile.

"Hey, Ben," Moki asked a few miles later, "How come your family doesn't live out at the ranch all the time?" Moki was notorious for asking personal questions. But embarrassing or not, his habit made him a good detective because he wasn't afraid to get to the heart of a situation.

"Gracie and I go to public school in Las Palmitas. And Mom's in town so she can find saddle club candidates. My dad goes back and forth once or twice a week from the Walnut Street house to the ranch to check on Aunt Maisie, the ranch workers, the horses, and our apple orchard. Then, we all go out there together once a month for a whole week with the next group of saddle club kids. Of course, our teachers send schoolwork with us."

"Cool," Moki replied. He gazed out the window at the beautiful sunny autumn day.

It was Ben's turn. "Lanny, why are you and Lexi home-schooled?"

"Our parents often travel for their jobs, and we go with them."

Rani added, "The twins have a live-in tutor named Bruce Wilding who's twenty-five years old. He teaches Moki and me, too, when we travel with them."

"Yeah, the guy's a genius," Moki said. "Lanny and I think he's a computer with legs."

"And the genius didn't forget to send this week's

lessons," Lexi replied with a smirk. She held up a canvas tote bag stuffed with books and papers.

Moki said, "Bruce does prepare cool lessons about whatever topic we're involved in."

Indeed, when Lanny looked through the pile of schoolwork Lexi had brought, he noticed sheets about the California Gold Rush of 1849—the '49ers, as those prospectors were called, gold since ancient times, and Cody's geology. There was even information on Papa Mayfield.

"I want to learn all those lessons, too," Gracie said from the row in front of the girls. She was truly interested in the material, but she was also determined to do most anything to stick close to the squad wherever possible during her special week at the ranch with the "celebrity" detectives.

"Sure thing," Lexi answered. "The more, the merrier. Catherine, Lionel, how about you?"

"I might be interested," Catherine replied in a level voice without turning to look at Lexi.

"Don't know yet," Lionel said without any eye contact. "What I do know is—my stomach is growling. And if I don't eat something right now, I'm gonna throw up."

Mrs. Mayfield took the not-so-subtle suggestion and passed around some granola bars and apples. A hush overtook the car as everyone ate. This gave the kids a chance to admire the scenery. It had turned from the resort town elegance of Las Palmitas to the slowly rising, rugged countryside. The landscape was becoming thick with oak, pepper, and pine trees. Sagebrush and boulder-strewn mountains lined the winding road to Cody. Rani pointed to a deer visible through some trees.

Catherine and Lionel gazed intently out the windows. They had never been outside the city before today. *Wish I was back home with my mama,* Catherine thought as she leaned against the car's interior and fought back tears.

Lionel was thinking, too, but scowling. *What am I doing here, anyway? Wish some of my friends could have come along. We'd really shake things up then.*

Ben noticed their silence. This was sadly too typical of some saddle club kids on the Monday drive. "It's going to be lots of fun at the ranch," he said to encourage them. "We get to hike, ride horses, camp out, play tennis, and swim."

"Really?" Catherine replied.

Ben noticed her slight smile, but no other reaction followed. And nothing from Lionel but a "hmph."

Soon, however, Catherine added, "Hey. That sign said 'Camel Dairy.' Camels, out here?"

Ben nodded.

"And ostrich and llama ranches, too," Gracie added.

Now, Catherine's and Lionel's eyes got big.

The snacks were gone by the time the van finished its climb, then started its slightly downward route through the mountain meadows and pine forests. The sun was momentarily blocked as the van wound around a mountain. Soon, however, the two-lane dirt road was speckled with late morning sun once again. Nearly two hours after leaving Las Palmitas, the travelers spotted a small town up ahead.

"Look, everybody. We're coming into Cody," Mr. Mayfield said as he accelerated.

The group noticed the tiny road sign that announced, "Historic Cody. Population 453. Elevation 4,200 feet." The two-lane, asphalt road accommodated weekend visitors—"city folks"—who loved coming for Cody's famous apple-berry pie, pine air, gold mine tours, and winter snow. Small stores and businesses, a bed-and-breakfast, and various restaurants lined the main street. It still looked like an authentic Old West town but now had all the modern conveniences. Being Monday, there were more horses hitched than cars parked in front of most businesses.

Lanny nudged Moki and pointed to the assay office they were passing on the left.

"Huh?" Moki said as he turned toward his friend.

"An assayer is a person who examines rock samples from prospectors wanting to stake a gold mine claim," Lanny explained.

Moki finally nodded and gave a thumbs up. It was a rare moment when he was happy for a definition from Lanny, who rarely missed a chance to provide one.

Ben added, "We can ride our horses back here tomorrow and visit that office."

"Perfect," Lanny said. "Plus a few other stops. I already have questions to ask regarding our case."

"Ten more minutes to the ranch," Mr. Mayfield sang

out. He sighed and grinned. "Boy, I'm looking forward to stretching my legs."

Within a minute, the van had left Cody behind and started a slow descent. The kids saw more trees than houses now. They passed by some apple orchards and small meadows with cows, horses, and sheep.

Catherine pointed out the window. "Whoa, look at that. I've never seen a real cow before."

"Yeah, only seen 'em in pictures," Lionel added with his fingers pressed against the window.

Soon, the group spotted a large, well-maintained ranch tucked into a shady meadow near the base of a mountain. Below the property, to the east, the flat desert spread out as far as the eye could see.

"Drum roll, please," Mrs. Mayfield said. Most of the kids slapped their legs rhythmically. "Announcing—we've arrived at Gold Mine Acres Ranch!"

Ben, Gracie, and the squad whooped and applauded. Soon, the van rolled under the old wooden entry arch and slowly passed the ranch house and the dark brown barn before stopping in front of a large, modern bunkhouse. Everyone climbed out, stretched, and inhaled the warm, sage-filled air that whooshed up from the desert. Around them, birds chirped, an occasional horse neighed, and the wind rustled through the oak trees.

Each person grabbed a suitcase or some gear and headed toward the building. Normally, Ben and Gracie slept in their own rooms at the ranch house. But this week, since there were only two saddle club guests plus the detective squad, Mrs. Mayfield had decided all the kids should stay together in the bunkhouse.

"Great idea," said Rani. "That way, Lexi and I can show Gracie and Catherine how to do henna tattoos."

Gracie jumped up and down, holding onto Rani's arm. Catherine's eyebrows raised.

Just inside the main door were two more doors. The one on the left led to the boys' bunks. Ben guided Moki, Lanny, and Lionel there. Gracie led Rani, Lexi, and Catherine through the right door. Mr. Mayfield followed Ben in and told the boys to choose their bunks and get ready for inspection. Mrs. Mayfield repeated the procedure to the girls.

Lexi was pleased by how clean and spacious their side of the bunkhouse was. At the back were restrooms, shower facilities, and sleeping quarters for the counselor, in this case, Mrs. Mayfield. Six kid cots smelled of fresh sheets and blankets. The girls chose their bunks with Gracie next to Rani and Catherine and Lexi across from them.

As the girls were settling in, Catherine whimpered, then suddenly burst into tears.

"What's wrong?" Lexi asked the girl whose face was buried in her bunk's pillow.

"I miss my mama." Catherine sat up and rubbed her eyes with balled-up fists.

"Catherine," said Mrs. Mayfield, hugging her. "Believe it or not, it won't be long before you'll be so involved in ranch life, you won't want to go home."

Gracie handed her tissues, and Catherine dabbed her eyes, slowly nodding. The other girls promised to help her.

Meanwhile, on the boys' side, Mr. Mayfield was conducting an inspection of the kids' suitcases and gear. He found a sack of candy bars in Lionel's belongings, which was taken away. Before the boy could complain, Moki said, "Dude, you don't want wildlife in your bed, do you?"

Lionel was silent for a few seconds. Then he glanced at the older boys. "Ugh! I admit it. I made a mistake. Mr. Mayfield, I'll try harder not to break the saddle clue rules again."

"Well, I'd say you've made an excellent start after all, young man," Mr. Mayfield replied.

Once everyone had freshened up, the Mayfield parents directed all the kids outside. Mrs. Mayfield pointed. "See those two rooms off the barn? That's where our two hired men stay. They have Sundays and Mondays off, but you'll meet them first thing tomorrow after breakfast. They'll mainly work with Catherine, Lionel, and the horses. I'll help, too."

Mr. Mayfield said, "Just so we're all clear, Catherine and Lionel, you two are here this week as our saddle club kids. That means you'll be doing different tasks from the other six kids and with more adult supervision. Mrs. Mayfield and I don't want you to feel like you're missing out on anything when the others head off on their own adventures. You two will have lots of adventures yourselves. Just different kinds."

"Yes," Mrs. Mayfield added. "And don't forget the other kids already know how to ride horses. You get to spend the week learning, among other fun activities. Got it?"

"Got it," both kids said together, heads bobbing.

Finally, the group walked toward the state-designated historic ranch house. It was an enormous two-story, brown wooden building with a covered porch. There was a bronze plaque near the front door commemorating the house being built by Papa Mayfield in 1875. Each generation of the proud family had carefully maintained the property and preserved its historical integrity.

A tall, older woman with short-cropped, curly gray hair and a chef's apron around her narrow waist held open the front door. "Come in, come in," she said brightly. She was introduced to the kids as Aunt Maisie. The woman smiled and shook hands with Lionel, Catherine, and the squad members, not forgetting to exchange hugs with Gracie and Ben. "Welcome to Gold Mine Acres Ranch. I bet you're all hungry as bears after that long drive."

Lionel boomed, "Yeeees, ma'am."

She let out a resounding laugh. "Well, you've come to the right place. Follow me." Aunt Maisie led the entire group through the homey living room and into the spacious dining room. A huge round table that could seat more than a dozen was set for ten for lunch. Above it was a rustic chandelier made from an old wagon wheel, festooned with electric candles in wrought iron holders. Black chains that gathered in the center suspended the entire fixture from the ceiling. Lexi smiled, thinking it gave the room the perfect Old West touch.

Mrs. Mayfield told the kids to look for their name cards above the luncheon plates. Those would indicate their permanent places at the table for the coming week. Soon, everyone was seated and inhaling the aromas that promised a delicious barbecued lunch.

Catherine and Lionel glanced at one another, then turned away abruptly when they discovered the other one didn't know what to do with their napkin. Instead, they imitated the others, placing the cloth across their laps.

Aunt Maisie had excused herself and gone into the kitchen to get the platters and bowls of food. But instead of the meal emerging, the kitchen erupted with Aunt Maisie's ear-splitting scream.

CHAPTER FIVE

· ✧ ·

Papa Mayfield's Treasure Box

At Aunt Maisie's scream, everyone raced from the dining room table into the kitchen, a few chairs getting knocked over in the process. A sight met their eyes. There in the middle of the room was a horse! Even funnier was Aunt Maisie. Now back to her normally fearless self, she was jumping up and down and pushing on the stocky animal. "I don't recall giving you permission to help me cook, let alone eat. Get yourself out of my clean kitchen this instant."

The startled horse obeyed, turned, and left the same way it had come in—through the enclosed back service porch and out the squeaky screen door. Finally, it plodded from the stoop into the backyard. Fortunately, neither kitchen nor food was harmed. The meticulous woman turned to the group and said, "I'm so sorry. I must have left the screen door unlatched, and Cookie thought that was her invitation to join the party."

"Whoa," said Lionel and Catherine, who had jumped

behind Moki and Lexi but slowly peeked out. Then everyone burst out laughing, including Aunt Maisie and the two saddle club kids. It couldn't have been a better ice breaker if it had been planned.

"Cookie's my horse," Gracie explained proudly. "She's a roan, which means she's a mix of white and colored hair on the top of her body, but mostly one dark color everywhere else."

Lionel's mouth fell open. "You . . . you mean you have your very own horse?"

"Yes, and now that you're a saddle club kid, you can come back and ride one whenever we're out here," Gracie replied. Her cheeks bunched up with her smile.

"But I don't think I want to ride," he replied. The boy's lower lip protruded, and his arms crisscrossed his chest in a tight hug.

Mrs. Mayfield said, "That's because you don't know how to ride yet, right?" She chuckled and gently pulled his chin up to face her. "You'll start learning tomorrow."

"Well . . . I'll give it a shot if I have to," the boy replied. His scowl had softened.

"Oh, and thanks for the accidental but important lesson, Aunt Maisie," Mr. Mayfield said. He turned to the kids. "That should teach each of you to always close doors behind you here at the ranch, or you might turn around and get a surprise."

Everyone nodded vigorously in agreement.

Moki scrunched up his nose and said, "Yeah, like a

snake with fangs of death. So, always—*always*, with a capital A—close those doors, please!"

Lexi and Rani rolled their eyes. They felt Moki purposely exaggerated his reptile phobia to get attention. Moki was afraid of snakes, no question, but *he* didn't feel it was abnormal. He had spent his boyhood in snake-free Hawai'i. In California, he had too quickly discovered that rattlesnakes were common in certain terrains, including the canyon adjacent to his house on Botanic Hill. He had no intention of encountering any, here or anywhere, if he could help it.

The group returned to the table and picked up their napkins and the overturned chairs. Gracie rejoined them after putting Cookie back into her corral. A discussion of the ranch's different kinds of horses occupied the lunch feast of barbecued-beef sandwiches, potato salad, green beans with bacon bits, a huge homemade apple pie—compliments of neighboring ranchers and friends Mr. and Mrs. Hollister—vanilla ice cream, and all the milk the kids could drink.

Catherine dug into her thick slice of pie, then touched Mrs. Mayfield's arm and whispered, "I think I'm already getting to like it here." The two exchanged big smiles.

After eating the last bite of pie on his plate, Lanny set his fork down and asked, "Mr. Mayfield, do you have any information here at the ranch about Papa Mayfield?"

"You must have read my mind, Lanny," he replied. "Ben and I are planning to show you detectives Papa's big treasure box as soon as you're finished eating."

Mrs. Mayfield said, "And Gracie and I thought we'd give Catherine and Lionel a tour of the ranch and then go swimming."

Gracie and Catherine nodded. Lionel gave two thumbs up.

"The rest of you are welcome to join us at the pool later if you like," she added. All agreed to the plan. A dip in the pool would be refreshing after their car ride.

Everyone thanked Aunt Maisie for the delicious meal. Once excused, the six older kids started clearing the table. Catherine and Lionel hung back but soon joined in before being told to help. Finally, Mrs. Mayfield and Gracie led the saddle club kids out the same back door Cookie had used. Mr. Mayfield and Ben led the detective squad into the large family room off the kitchen.

"You called the box a 'treasure box,' Mr. Mayfield," Rani said. "Why is that?"

"Well, Rani, that's the name our family gave it generations ago. Papa made the box himself and stored his valuable papers and photos inside—historical treasures, you might say."

"But not the gold mine claim," Lanny said, looking from Mr. Mayfield to Ben.

"No, unfortunately, not the gold mine claim," Ben repeated with a head shake. "We've searched through the box many times, but it's not in there."

Mr. Mayfield opened a low cabinet and brought out a large wooden box. It did, indeed, look like an old pirate treasure chest. The rusty hinges creaked as he opened the heavy lid. A strong, musty odor filled the room, but it was soon forgotten when the actual contents were revealed.

"Here are more photos and some drawings of my five-time great-grandfather," Ben said as he handed each detective items from the box. "Photography was a new invention back then."

"Wow, Papa was tall," Rani said as she gazed at a photo.

"And handsome and well dressed," Lexi added. "There's his deputy marshal star on his vest. And here's one of him kind of dirty, but still well dressed, especially for a miner."

"Papa remains a legend among Black people here in California," Mr. Mayfield said. "He brought himself a long way from being born a slave on a Georgia cotton plantation. Most slaves were freed in 1865, after the Civil War, so he went to Northern California intending to mine for gold."

Ben added, "As he traveled west, Papa taught himself how to shoot pistols and rifles, and he became an expert marksman. Lawmen noticed his skills and offered Papa the deputy marshal job to bring law and order to the gold mine camps. He became one of the first Black deputy U.S. marshals in California before he ever had a chance to do much gold mining."

"A true *paniolo*, and then some," Moki said.

Ben continued, "Yes, he was one first-rate cowboy, all right. Papa even used disguises to trap outlaws. And he was an excellent horseback rider who preferred to bring in fugitives alive instead of dead. He collected a five thousand dollar reward for capturing and delivering just one outlaw."

"Wow!" Lanny said with a whistle. "That's a lot of money, especially for back then. How many criminals did he bring in during his career?"

"Over two thousand felons," Ben said, "and all but ten were brought in alive. It was said Papa had a way of 'charming' the outlaws into giving up."

"That's a heap of charm and a whole lot of reward money, dude," Moki said.

Mr. Mayfield replied, "He was a rich man before he ever came to Cody, and his gold mine here made him even richer. We thank him daily for our family's continued abundance."

"Was he ever hurt while capturing outlaws?" Lexi asked.

"Never shot," Ben replied. "His tall, old white hat got shot a few times, though." Ben grinned. Then, he pulled a heavy cloth bag from the box. From it, he handed out an object wrapped in special paper—Papa's well-preserved hat.

The kids noticed five bullet holes in the top. Moki started to put his finger through one of the holes, but Lexi pulled his hand back.

Moki said, "Wow. Close calls. He was lucky. . . . We're all lucky. If anything had happened to Papa, we wouldn't be here today admiring him and working on a mystery."

Everyone smiled and agreed.

"I saved the best for last," Ben said. He removed the lid from a small gray square box. Inside was Papa's deputy marshal badge.

The detectives sighed as they gazed at the shiny old brass star.

Lanny put his attention back on some documents he had been carefully studying. Papa had written and signed them himself. The boy asked, "So, Papa knew how to read and write?"

"More of his remarkable skills," Mr. Mayfield said. "It was against the law in the mid-1800s in America to teach slaves how to read and write, but Papa's father taught him anyway, probably in secret at night with the pages lit up as they sat next to the fireplace."

Another hour was spent discussing every item in the treasure box until it was empty. The kids lingered over the photos, old bank account ledgers, and store receipts that made them feel as if they had been transported back in time. None of the photos showed the gold mine, much to Lanny's dismay. But the group had fun reading a Cody general store receipt from Papa's purchase of a pickaxe for ten cents, a shovel for a quarter, and a kerosene lantern for one dollar. It was dated May 15, 1878. Rani remarked that those items were likely used by Papa for gold mining right here on the ranch.

The Mayfields' smiles showed their family pride.

Lanny glanced inside the box. His sharp detective eyes saw a miniscule wooden knob on the bottom off to one corner. It would have been easy to miss had the box not been in the right light. The Mayfields had never noticed the knob before and gave Lanny permission to pull on it.

Lanny couldn't get his fingers around the awkwardly positioned knob, so Rani tried. With her smaller hand, she succeeded. After barely a yank, the bottom of the box popped upward. Six heads quickly circled above the container as everyone looked inside at a hidden compartment.

A cloth was wedged into the space. After some jiggling, Ben managed to lift it out. He noticed it contained something heavy. But an object in the bottom of the box distracted him momentarily. It was a soiled, rumpled photo, which he handed to his dad. Then, Ben quickly unwrapped the cloth. It contained an enormous, blackened iron skeleton key. He traced over its ornate top section. But still no gold mine claim was to be found.

Mr. Mayfield whistled. "Well, I'll be. Could these objects really have remained hidden all these years since Papa placed them there?"

Lanny replied, "Maybe he intentionally wrapped the key to keep it from rattling around inside the box. That could account for why these weren't discovered until now."

"What do you see in the photo, Dad?" Ben asked as he craned his neck to look.

The man lowered the photo so the others could see. "It's another picture of Papa, but this time, it looks as if he's with a couple of fellow miners. They're holding hand tools and look to be standing in front of a cave, given the large dark space behind them." Mr. Mayfield slowly smiled. This was, indeed, a significant discovery.

"If that's Papa's gold mine," Moki replied, "we have a terrific clue to its actual existence and its appearance."

"And perhaps to its location," Rani added. "Those trees in the photo could be landmarks. They look fairly small in the photo. So maybe they're mature now and still on the property."

"How about the key?" Lexi asked, gesturing to Ben, who was holding it up to his face, studying it closely.

Ben said, "It looks super old to me. These are cut-out designs on top. Definitely a skeleton key." He handed it first to Lexi.

"Heavy," she said. "Since the photo and the key were hidden together, they must be related somehow."

"That's certainly logical," Lanny said. "If the mine had a door, maybe the key opened it."

Lexi replied, "Good thinking, Lanny. Too bad the miners are standing in front of the cave—or mine—and blocking our view."

Moki added, "But if it had a door, and if the door still exists, we could have another clue to help us tell Papa's mine from an ordinary cave."

"Good call, bro," Lanny replied.

Mr. Mayfield handed the photo to a beaming Lanny and said, "This is a big discovery. Thank you, everyone. I'm impressed with your ideas. I'm entrusting the photo and the key to all of you for your investigation this week."

After the treasure box's contents were carefully returned and the box stowed once again in the cabinet, the kids headed to the bunkhouse where Lanny secured the photo and key. Then, they changed for an afternoon swim and joined the others already enjoying the large, inviting turquoise pool.

Moki showed Catherine and Lionel how to cannonball off the diving board. A contest resulted to see who could splash the most water out of the pool and drench Mrs. Mayfield, reclining on a chaise lounge. She took it all in stride.

As dinnertime approached, everyone headed to the bunkhouse for dry clothes. Soon, they took themselves and their big appetites to the ranch house and found their places at the table. Aunt Maisie had prepared another feast, this time of green salad, oven-roasted chicken and vegetables, buttermilk biscuits, mashed potatoes, and sliced, ranch-grown fresh fruit for dessert.

After the scrumptious dinner and cleanup, all the kids stepped out to stand on the large front porch.

"Check out that gorgeous almost-full moon rising over the desert." Lexi sighed, pointing, as she leaned into the railing.

"That's a waxing gibbous moon," Lanny said. "It will be full in a few days."

Rani replied, "You're so smart. You should be a teacher when you grow up."

Moki laughed. "*If* he grows up! He had to duck a jab to his jaw from Lanny.

The land seemed magically illuminated for miles to the east and north, and millions of stars were visible in the inky night sky. The air still smelled of sage from the warm autumn day. A stillness and peace had descended upon the scene, making everyone feel as if they were in some make-believe world. The magic was intensified when, from some distant place, first one coyote whooped, then seconds later, another answered.

Lionel sighed and said, "Ah, this is the life. . . . Never imagined I'd say that!"

Catherine looked as if she had melted onto the porch railing, with her hands cupping a support beam. "It's peaceful in the country at night, isn't it? More than in the city. That's for sure." She smiled as her eyes closed.

Moki jumped up. "Hey, what's that hissing sound? Don't tell me snakes . . ."

"Relax, dude. Just desert crickets," Ben replied. "They hiss instead of chirp out here."

Lexi said, "Chill, Moki. You're disturbing the peace."

If the Phantom Rider rode that night, none of the kids were aware. Sleep had overpowered them soon after moongazing, and the comfortable cots assisted their slumber. It had been a memorable first day at Gold Mine Acres Ranch and Youth Saddle Club. Tomorrow would be filled with new adventures and horseback riding for all.

And Lanny was anxious to get to Cody.

CHAPTER SIX

· ✧ ·

Horseback Ride to Cody

Ben's parents rang the wake-up bell loudly the next morning at seven o'clock. Roosters from ranches near and far seemed to be having a crowing contest to welcome the Tuesday sunlight streaming through the bunkhouse windows.

The boys found the girls already at the breakfast table by the time they got to the ranch house. The meal was presented buffet style. Aunt Maisie was overseeing her young guests as they made healthy choices with reasonable portion sizes. Moki was assured he could come back for seconds as long as he had eaten everything on his plate. He told the cook politely that finishing all his food was never a problem. Lexi's and Rani's vigorous nods confirmed this.

A short time later, the last buffet dish had been scraped clean, a testament to Aunt Maisie's great cooking and the kids' hearty appetites.

Mr. Mayfield asked, "Is anyone ready to start riding horses this morning?"

"Yee-haw!" Moki replied. He had dressed in his version of a Hawaiian *paniolo* outfit, complete with a Hawaiian shirt, bandana, blue jeans, and boots. The others were also in western clothes, including Rani, who wisely knew saris and horses didn't mix.

Each kid grabbed their hat from the living room hatstand, made their way out the front door, and aimed for the riding arena. It was well beyond the bunkhouse, swimming pool, and tennis courts.

"I'm kind of nervous about the horses," Catherine said as she frowned up at Lexi.

"That's natural," Lexi replied, taking the girl's hand. "But take it nice and slow, and you'll be riding around the arena in no time. The helpers will guide you. And they'll start with easy riding techniques. That's how Lanny and I learned."

"Really?" Catherine's face relaxed. So did her grasp on Lexi's hand.

Mrs. Mayfield added, "Lexi is correct. But first, all of you need to meet our trainers." She led the group over to the huge fenced arena with a few bleachers flanking it. There were two men inside the sand-filled showground. Eight horses, already saddled and awaiting riders, stood side by side at the fence. Some whinnied and pawed at the ground.

"Here are our trainers," the woman said with a broad smile and outstretched arm. "Mr. Hume Jaxton and Mr. Rufus Crawford."

The men shook hands with each of the kids and repeated their names.

Moki smirked and added, "Lanny's real name is 'Lanyon,' and Lexi's is 'Alexia.'"

"But just call me Lanny," the boy said after elbowing his friend in the ribs.

"And please call me Lexi," she said, glowering at Moki.

Mr. Jaxton smiled and added, "Welcome to all of you. Just call me Jax. I'll be teaching the saddle club kids how to ride a horse." He was a tall, muscular man, about forty years old, who seemed friendly. His battered cowboy hat was tilted back, revealing his high fade haircut. His dark forehead was already glistening with perspiration.

"And you can call me Rufus," Mr. Crawford said. "No 'mister,' please. Just Rufus. I'll mainly be teaching you how to take care of your horse." The hired hand was younger and shorter than Jax, but also burly. He had strong arms, leathery hands, and close-cropped, wavy black hair.

Lionel replied, "Well, you can call me Lion. That's what my friends nicknamed me."

"And I like to be called Cat," Catherine said more softly.

Jax threw his head back and laughed, saying, "Well, so we have two members of the feline family with us this week."

Lionel didn't reply, having already turned his attention to the ponies. "Can we choose our own horse?"

Jax grinned. "Within limits. Some are better for first-time riders like you and Cat."

Everyone knew Cookie was Gracie's horse. Ben went over and led his horse toward the group. "This is my horse. He's a palomino. That's a horse with a gold coat and a white mane and white tail. His name is Jet, and boy, does he ever live up to his name." The others patted Jet, who bobbed his head vigorously, snorted, and pawed his welcome.

Within a few minutes, the horses and riders were paired. Lionel would ride Zippy, a piebald quarter horse that, unlike Jet, did not live up to his name. Catherine was happy with a chestnut quarter horse, Bella. Lanny would be on a gray Arabian named Sam. Lexi patted her stallion, a light coppery sorrel named Toby. And Rani already liked her strawberry roan filly, Ginger.

Moki approached the last horse, a bay, with black mane, tail, and shorter legs. "So Jax, what's my mare's name?"

"That's Grandma," the man said with a grin.

Moki's face fell as everyone laughed.

"Hey, now, don't you worry one bit, Moki," Jax reassured him, patting the horse that apparently had a special place in the trainer's heart. "Grandma's one of our most spirited horses. I heard you did a lot of riding in Hawai'i, so I think you'll be able to handle her."

"Strange name for a spunky horse," the boy said under his breath as he took her reins.

Ben nudged his friend. "Dude, Grandma got her name because, as a foal, she looked like an old soul. You'll see that's as far as the comparison goes when you start riding her."

"Hmm," replied Moki. "Time will tell, dude. Time will tell."

Ben, Gracie, and the detectives led their horses through the arena gate, wished Catherine and Lionel a fun day, and mounted for a brisk ride to Cody. All six were excellent riders. Lexi turned and gave Catherine a thumbs up. The girl smiled back and waved. Mrs. Mayfield wished them safe and happy trails. Then she took a seat in a bleacher to help Jax and Rufus work with the saddle club kids after thoroughly slathering Catherine's freckled arms and face and Lionel's dark skin with sunscreen, despite the boy's protests. The club kids put on their required helmets and were ready at last.

As the other six kids headed away from the arena, they could hear Jax and Rufus giving Catherine and Lionel the usual Tuesday morning talk about the saddle club rules and some important safety precautions around horses. Gracie was beaming as she sat taller than usual in her saddle. She knew the investigation was getting underway, and she was definitely now a part of it.

Ben was in the lead and glanced back as the riders skillfully began the slow climb from the ranch up the mountain trail that led to Cody. It was obvious to him that the others were well matched with their horses. Moki even had Grandma in hand. Horses and riders had bonded almost immediately.

Ben had wisely come to realize since they left Las Palmitas how important it was for his sister to be included with the squad. He liked to set a good example around saddle club kids, so he hadn't put up a fuss when Gracie came with them this morning. Still, deep down, he wasn't exactly happy about her horning in. *It's only for this one week,* he said to calm himself.

In about fifteen minutes, the desert, ranch, and meadows were far behind them as pine and oak forests overtook the terrain. Rani breathed in deeply and said, "It smells like Christmas!" Everyone agreed.

There were no cars vying for the road today, so the ride was smooth and fast. Lexi and Rani enjoyed their horses and the shadow-play on the trail as the sunlight was briefly eclipsed by enormous tree branches. Lanny patted Sam and deeply inhaled the cool, fresh pine air as questions for the morning's investigation in town whirled in his head.

Ten minutes later, Ben announced, "We're coming into Cody."

Six horseback riders entering town was not unusual, so some residents on the main street merely nodded or waved hello when they saw the kids clip-clopping along.

A smiling woman had just gotten off her horse and waved. "Hey, Ben and Gracie. Great to see you two back in town. Need any supplies for the ranch today?"

"No, thanks, Ms. Annie," Ben called back. "Not today. But it's great to see you, too." He turned around to the detectives. "That's Annie Banks. She owns Cody's general store. She used to let Gracie and me pick out free candy from her barrels when we were little kids."

Ben led the group to the assay office since that was where, the day before, Lanny had indicated he wanted to go. The hitching post was sufficient for tying up all six horses after the detectives dismounted.

Moki rubbed his backside. "Whoa! Feels good to get off that horse for a bit."

"I bet *Captain Jack Sparrow* is a great horseback rider who would never complain about being in the saddle," Lexi replied with a smirk.

"Huh?" Gracie said, leaning back and hiking her eyebrows in confusion.

"Let me explain," Lexi replied with a chuckle. "Moki thinks he's the Hawaiian Captain Jack Sparrow . . . you know, from the pirate movies."

"Ohh, I get it now," Gracie said. "Hmm." After checking the boy out for a few seconds, she added, shaking her index finger, "You know, Moki, you do look a little bit like a pirate. You need straggly pirate hair with golden trinkets and shells in it. And you're way too clean."

"Arrghh!" Moki said in her face. "'Bring me that horizon'—I mean, assay office."

Getting down to business, the group approached the office, only to bump shoulders with a tall plaid-shirted man just coming out. It was Nate Seeley, the head cook at The Cody Café.

"Well, I'll be," he said, slapping his knee. "If it isn't the Mayfield kids come to town. How's life been treatin' ya?" Before they could answer, he added, "Got some new items on the menu you should try this trip. Bring your parents in, and Aunt Maisie, too."

"Hi, Mr. Nate," Gracie replied. "Life's great, thanks! I'll ask my parents about all of us maybe coming for lunch soon."

After a few more seconds of conversation with Mr. Seeley, the kids said their good-byes to him and entered the office. They immediately spotted a beefy, middle-aged man in a cowboy hat sitting at a desk behind the big front counter. His nameplate identified him as "Parker Wells, Assayer."

"Well, hello, Ben and Gracie," Mr. Wells said over the top of his newspaper as he rocked in his squeaky wooden chair. "What brings you kids in here today? And who are your friends?"

"Hi, Mr. Wells," Ben said with a wave.

He and Gracie introduced the detectives by their names but left out their detective titles. During their ride, Lanny had asked them not to draw attention to their case. "We have some questions for you." Ben looked at Lanny, who took his cue.

The boy got right to the point. "Mr. Wells, we're wondering if you have a record of the claim for Papa Mayfield's mine from the 1870s."

Instead of answering Lanny, Parker Wells slowly pushed himself away from his desk, stood, and turned to Ben. "Now, Ben, your family has been in here before asking about that. As promised, I've continued to search, but I'm sorry to report there doesn't seem to be any record of such a claim. And remember, there was a fire here many years ago, long before computer files. A number of records were lost. I suspect Papa's was among them."

Lanny stood tall. "But if a gold mine is on someone's property, doesn't that person or family automatically have a claim on it?"

Mr. Wells hesitated for a second. "No," he said slowly, eyeing the boy. "Even if the mine is on your property, it doesn't mean you have exclusive and legal rights to mine the minerals there. It's always a good idea to stake a claim to be on the safe side."

"'Safe side'?" Rani asked. She drummed her impatient fingertips on the counter.

"It's a good idea to file a mining claim to protect your investment if you intend to do any serious mining, little lady. Otherwise, someone else might claim or have already claimed a legal mining right you don't have or don't know about. Also, it might be determined that the mine isn't on the person's property after all." He pursed his lips and crossed his arms over his barrel chest.

"Can claims be bought or transferred?" Moki asked, ignoring the man's body language.

"Yes, they can be bought, leased, traded, or transferred," he replied quickly.

"With the original owner's knowledge, of course," Lanny added.

Wells nodded slowly and pushed his hat back off his forehead, revealing his thick blond hair, and looked down his nose at the boy.

Then, Rani remembered a question her father had suggested and asked Mr. Wells about Cody's gold-bearing productive rock types—meaning the most common types of rocks where gold might be found. The assayer looked surprised at her question but confirmed quartz, granite, and schist would likely be found near a Cody gold mine. This corroborated what Rani's father had told her.

Wells quickly added with a slight smirk, "Too bad there aren't any gold mine tours conducted on weekdays this time of year, or you could see that for yourselves. Can't even get near the mines 'til Saturday. Gates are locked."

The assayer also confirmed Rani's dad's information that there were currently eight gold mine claims staked in the area. He pointed them out on the wall map behind them. "Notice none of them is on Gold Mine Acres Ranch? No mining there anymore, I'm afraid. Too bad."

Lanny was itching to follow up with a comment to the effect that it wouldn't matter then if they decided to try to find Papa's mine, but common sense, instinct, and a good upbringing told him not to say another word or reveal any of their plans to this contrary man.

"Say, what makes you kids so interested in mining, anyway?" he asked as if reading Lanny's mind. His arms were still crossed over his puffed-out chest, and he stood tall, purposely gazing down on them.

Rani replied calmly, "It seems natural to wonder about that given that Cody is a historic gold mining town. Don't you agree, Mr. Wells?"

The assayer eyed the kids but didn't reply.

The group thanked the assayer and left the office.

No sooner were they outside when Rani said, "He called me 'little lady'—hmph!"

She kicked a stone off the porch, sending it skittering into the street.

"There are a few reasons to be upset with him, BFF, including that," Lexi said, giving Rani a sideways hug. "I don't think he was nice or helpful at all."

Lanny was also annoyed but mostly puzzled, and for a different reason.

After they walked a few steps, Moki asked him what was wrong.

Lanny said, "You know, Mr. Wells never mentioned that a claim's boundaries have to be physically staked in the ground with a monument marker sign."

Moki's eyebrows raised. "Maybe he didn't know— Nah. He knew."

Lexi replied, "Maybe he didn't think it was important for our purposes."

Rani looked hard at the others and said, "Maybe he didn't *want* us to know."

CHAPTER SEVEN

· ✧ ·

Horse Sense and the Law

The kids were mulling over their meeting with Cody's snarky assayer and his snide comments when Lanny spotted the veterinarian's office. He pointed his thumb at the rustic-looking building a few steps away. "Let's go in there. I have some questions for the doctor."

The kids stepped into an empty but inviting waiting room decorated with horse-themed wallpaper. At the front desk was a huge vase of wildflowers, and orange hard-plastic chairs with shiny chrome legs were scattered around the room's perimeter. Ben asked the cheerful receptionist if Dr. Jameson was in and available to meet with them.

Momentarily, a fit, tanned, middle-aged woman named Dr. Cassie Jameson—according to the name tag pinned to her green scrubs—appeared. She knew the Mayfields well since she had cared for their ranch animals over the years. "Hi, Ben and Gracie. Who are your friends?"

Introductions were made.

"Are the horses okay?"

"Oh sure. They're all fine," Ben said.

"Then what can I do for you?"

Lanny picked up the conversation. "Horses—actually, one horse—is why we're here. Dr. Jameson, do you happen to know who might own a tall white Arabian stallion?"

"I think the horse you're referring to is named Lightning," the veterinarian replied.

Lexi sucked in her breath. The woman now had all six kids' full attention.

"I don't know its owner, however, since he or she doesn't live in Cody or nearby as far as I know."

Lexi stifled a groan.

"That's what we're trying to find out," Lanny replied. "How do you know Lightning?"

"I recently overheard some locals in the café across the street talking about a white Arabian stallion someone thought was named Lightning. The horse had been spotted galloping northeast across the desert, seemingly without a rider."

Ben instantly exchanged glances with the squad members.

"Could be the horse is wild or abandoned," the veterinarian added.

"Did they say anything else about that?" Ben wanted to know.

"No," Dr. Jameson said, shaking her head, her thick brown ponytail flapping side to side. "Nothing more about the horse's name or its possible owner. As I recall, the subject was dropped."

"Who were some of the people in the café that were talking about Lightning?" Gracie asked. Rani gave her a thumbs-up for a great question, which caused the girl to grin ear to ear.

"Well, let's see." The veterinarian bit her lip and looked up at the ceiling for a second. "A few local ranchers . . . oh, and I distinctly remember the sheriff and his deputy being there."

"That's good information," Lanny replied. "I have another question, doctor. Can a purebred horse and its owner be traced through a horse registry?"

"Usually, if the horse was registered. Sometimes, owners even register their horse in a specific breed association. But some horses that are registered can be difficult to trace since their owners might change the horse's name, ownership, or location and not update the records. And some owners don't apply, because they don't anticipate breeding the horse. In other words, they figure they won't recoup the application cost, so why bother?"

"Could that be true of a cowboy who uses his horse strictly for riding?" Moki asked.

"Well . . . yes, I could see that being a possible reason not to apply."

"We would appreciate it if you could please check if Lightning is registered," Lanny replied. "Specifically, we would like to find out who his owner is and where that person lives. I looked online about horse registries in general, but I quickly learned that I didn't know enough to have any luck."

"I'd be happy to look into it and call you with my findings," the veterinarian replied. "Sounds as if one of you is in the market for an Arabian."

The kids smiled but said nothing.

She quickly added, "Oh, and I'll check with our local farrier to see if she's ever shod a white Arabian stallion or trimmed his feet."

Lexi looked confused.

"Allow me to be the wordsmith today," Moki said since he had much more experience with horses than the other detectives. "A 'farrier' is someone who puts horseshoes on horses, and 'shod' means to shoe a horse. Arabians have naturally hard feet and don't always wear shoes, but their hooves still need filing, or trimming." He turned to Lanny. "Right, bro?"

Everyone looked at "Lanny the Lexicon," who had a reputation for defining words without request. This time, Moki had beaten him to it.

"Whatever you say, Bro Wordsmith," Lanny replied. The two exchanged smirks. The group thanked the doctor for her help, said they would look forward to her phone call, and left.

"Where to next, Sherlock?" Lexi asked her brother. Sherlock Holmes was Lanny's favorite British, fictional detective, and he often patterned his detection methods after the famous character. Plus, with two of his grandparents being English, he felt he was more than entitled to channel that part of his heritage.

Ben answered for Lanny. "We can go wherever you guys want, but first, I'd like to introduce you to the sheriff. He's a great guy."

"That's exactly where I wanted to go next," Lanny replied.

The others nodded. Ben led the group across the street, all quiet except for an occasional horse snorting.

Gracie opened the sheriff's office door. The group was greeted by two men—Sheriff Cliff Buckley, sitting behind his desk, and his deputy, Ned Buchanan, standing next to him. Both were middle-aged, burly men, also in cowboy hats. Moki was now convinced that being tall and muscular and owning a hat were required for being an adult Cody resident. Lanny thought the office was right out of a Western movie, except for the telephone, computer, and other tech tools scattered around the room.

"Well, well. Ben and Gracie Mayfield. Good to see you two again," Sheriff Buckley said with flashing pale blue eyes. He was immediately on his feet, reaching across the counter, and extending his hand to the two. He smiled broadly despite a badly sunburned face. "Who are your friends?"

Ben introduced them, again remembering Lanny's warning not to mention to anyone that the squad members were detectives.

"Did you come to see your many-time great-grandfather's picture again?" Ned Buchanan asked as he lifted his hat, scratched his rumpled strawberry-blond hair, then returned the hat to his head.

Gracie smiled and nodded.

"It's still on the wall right where it's always been," Sheriff Buckley said, pointing behind him. The kids gathered around it. There, indeed, was a smaller version of the picture they had seen in the Mayfields' study on Walnut Street.

The sheriff continued, "You know, he's always been a kind of hero of mine."

The deputy asked, "So, Ben, are these your friends or saddle club kids?"

"Friends. We had room in the van since only two saddle club kids wanted to come."

"It's too bad more kids aren't taking advantage of the great opportunity your parents are providing at the ranch," the sheriff said with a head shake.

Ben shrugged and replied as politely as he could, "Maybe if we find out who's been stealing things from the ranch, it'll get more families back on board."

The sheriff frowned. "Any more thefts out there since my last visit?"

"Yes," Ben replied, then sighed. "Jax, our hired hand, told my dad this morning that more bridles and some spurs were taken last night. Dad's going to call you about it later today to report it. Oh, and here's another note the thief left. It was tacked to the barn door." Ben handed the note to the sheriff, who observed that it was made from letters cut out and glued to a piece of dirty, crumpled paper like the last one. It read, "Get out now, or next, you will be injured!"

"This is very threatening and disturbing," the sheriff said with a frown as he studied the note before handing it to the deputy to inspect.

Lanny seized the opportunity. "Sheriff Buckley, Deputy Buchanan, do either of you know about a horse named—" but that's as far as he got. The office door suddenly burst open, and in stormed the assayer, Parker Wells, with a few leaves swirling in behind him.

Without looking around the room, Wells blurted, "We need to talk about—" but when he saw the kids, his face fell. He stopped speaking as abruptly as he had entered, and his face instantly flushed crimson.

"Hey, Parker," the sheriff said to the startled man. "Good morning. We were just talking to Ben's friends here. Have you met them yet?"

"Yeah, a bit ago. . . . Pleased to see all of you again," he stammered.

The sheriff said, "Well, kids, we'll have to catch up another time. Looks as if business calls. Back to work for us lawmen. Oh, and Ben, please tell your parents I would be happy to come out to the ranch and teach the saddle club kids how to play chess. Kids having positive experiences with police officers and vice versa are important. Another great idea of your mother's." The sheriff smiled as he escorted them to the door. "Come again!"

The group reluctantly followed the sheriff. Lanny shuffled out last, not happy he wasn't able to ask the sheriff or the deputy if they knew anything about Lightning. But the shocked look on the assayer's red face when he saw the kids left no doubt in Lanny's mind that the trip into Cody had already proven worthwhile to their investigation.

CHAPTER EIGHT

· ✧ ·

Important Ranch Discussions

The group's ride back to the ranch from town was uneventful. To pass the time, Moki brought up one of his favorite subjects, food. This naturally segued into what Lexi bragged was Rani's special ability, synesthesia.

"What's synes—whatever Lexi said?" Ben asked.

Rani replied, "Synesthesia is an unusual mixing of the senses, an extrasensory ability where one type of brain stimulation, let's say, hearing or reading a word or name, makes you experience something else. In my case, that something else is a taste or smell. The official name of my ability is *lexical-gustatory*—meaning 'word to taste'—synesthesia."

Moki pulled his horse up to Ben's and whispered so Gracie, riding farther ahead, wouldn't hear. "When you told us after the party the other day that the Phantom Rider had worn a mask, it made Rani taste mac 'n' cheese. That's what she tastes when she hears the word 'mask.'"

"Actually, I've been craving mac 'n' cheese ever since," Rani replied quietly. "I'm still hoping this mystery will ramp up and get the flavor off my mind and taste buds."

"Okay, so, uh . . . what's my name make you taste?" Ben asked.

"Ben—couscous," Rani answered immediately.

"Huh?" Ben's eyebrows knitted together. "What's 'couscous'? Is it a good thing?"

"Dude, we need to do some serious cooking," Moki replied. "It's a healthy kind of pasta. It makes a great side dish. Oh, and FYI, synesthesia isn't fatal. And it isn't contagious, either."

Gracie was now tuned in. "How about my name?"

"Grapes, the green seedless kind, but especially the skins."

"Cool," said Gracie. "I like all kinds of grapes, even the skins. I don't peel my grapes. Mom says they have more vitamins that way."

"Peel grapes! Who does that?" Lexi laughed with hiked eyebrows.

"Only rich people," Moki replied. "They have their servants do it for them."

Lexi said, "Moki, you just reminded me of something. Hey, Lanny, wasn't the line, 'Peel me a grape,' in one of your old Hollywood movies from the 1930s? Who was that actress who said that? . . . Oh yeah, Mae West."

But Lanny, who didn't often miss an opportunity to discuss movies from Hollywood's Golden Era, hadn't heard the conversation or the questions. He was deep in thought and looked forward to returning to the ranch where they could discuss the Cody trip findings face to face.

They reached the ranch on time at three o'clock. After all six horses were cared for and stabled, the kids headed for the bunkhouse. The squad's talk would have to wait until later since Catherine and Lionel were there with the Mayfield parents, sitting in the shade at the large, outdoor picnic table. They were discussing what they had learned on their first day as saddle club kids. The snacks of cheddar cheese cubes, pretzel rods, and ice-cold orange juice further enticed Moki to join the group. Lunch for the Cody visitors had been peanut butter and jelly sandwiches, squished from being stored in their saddle bags, plus bruised apples, and lukewarm water guzzled from their canteens.

Catherine jumped up and grabbed Lexi's hand, leading her to the table. "I only fell off Bella twice today," she said, holding up two fingers, "but I got back on her both times."

Lexi smiled down at her and thought how much Catherine had changed from the angry, sulky girl she had met just three days ago.

"And the fact that you got back up each time was important," Edie Mayfield said. "What else did you learn from that?"

"That if you fall down seven times, you stand up eight," the girl replied with a smile.

"That's from a Native-American proverb," Lionel added. "We have to remember that when life knocks us down."

Lexi replied, "Wow, you guys learned a lot today, and it's only day one."

Rani added, "And every time you stand up, you'll be stronger."

"Yup," Lionel replied, now with a pretzel rod clinched in each fist and poised on his head to look like horns. He turned, grimaced at the others, and made snorting sounds.

Lanny laughed. "Aww, a lion with horns. Scary! But what did you two learn about riding a horse?" He and the others were now seated around the table, giving the saddle club kids competition for the snacks.

Catherine replied, "Well, we learned how to get up on a horse—I mean, mount—how to hold the reins, how to keep our feet in the stirrups, how to dismount safely, and how to make friends with our horses."

"Yeah, like brushing them. And it helps to feed them apples, carrots, and sugar cubes," Lionel replied.

"So, it sounds as if you like horses now," Moki said, looking from Catherine to Lionel.

"Do we ever," Catherine replied. "I'm not afraid of them anymore. Especially now that I know about them and how to respect them and be careful around them."

Lionel nodded his agreement. "Yeppers to that."

"Again, that's a lot like life, wouldn't you say?" Ezra Mayfield asked the two. "The more you get to know someone or something, the easier it is to figure them out. Then you can decide if it's a good idea to respect them and make friends with them."

The two kids nodded some more.

Lionel hesitated, then added, "You know, today, I decided I've made friends with too many people before I've really gotten to know them."

Moki thought how good it was that some of the boy's rough edges were already being polished smooth. "Atta boy," Moki said. The two fist-bumped.

"Lion, I'd say you've come a long way already," Edie Mayfield added. "Good job." She gave him a sideways hug, and he didn't pull away.

Catherine added, "Yeah, my mom says it's the quality, not the quantity, of your friends that's important." It was her and Lexi's turn to fist-bump.

"And she's so right," Mrs. Mayfield replied. "Thanks for adding that."

The snacks had disappeared fast. Mr. and Mrs. Mayfield told Lionel and Catherine it was time to head for the bunkhouse to clean up and have some quiet reading and relaxing time. Ben and Gracie were reminded to go clean up, too, then help Aunt Maisie prepare dinner. The detectives offered to help in the kitchen as well but asked if they could have a few minutes to talk privately first. The idea was approved, and the others headed off to their own tasks. This left the squad alone at the table with a welcome chance to share their thoughts about the Cody visit.

"So, guys, let's run it down," Lanny began. He was standing with one foot on the bench, leaning into the group. This was his usual way of starting a meeting to sort information, gather everyone's ideas, and chart a course for further investigating.

The four discussed the people they had met that day to determine who were "persons of interest," meaning people to watch or question again who might know about the Arabian stallion, the Phantom Rider, the missing ranch items, or the gold mine's location.

"I know one thing's for sure," Moki said, frowning and flexing his arm muscle. "I'd need to gain weight and pump more iron before I'd want to meet Parker Wells in a dark barn."

"Keep eating the way you have been at the ranch, and it'll happen," Lexi replied.

"And hope Mr. Wells had learned some good manners before you got to that barn, dude," Lanny added with an eye roll.

Rani said quickly, "I thought Dr. Jameson was nice and helpful. I hope she discovers that Lightning is registered. We just might find out who the Phantom Rider is—the easy way."

"What would be the hard way?" Lexi asked.

"Having to lasso him and pull him off his horse to unmask him," Rani said with a chuckle. Then, she sat up straight. "Which reminds me. We need to make some mac 'n' cheese."

The others laughed until Lanny brought them back to their task. "It's too bad the vet has never treated Lightning."

Lexi replied, "She may not know him or his owner, but at least she told us what the horse's name might be and confirmed what Ben told us about a white Arabian stallion that seemed to gallop without a rider."

"And it appears Lightning has become a legend around here," Moki said.

"Then, let's keep our ears and eyes open for who else might know about the horse," Lanny replied. "And maybe Dr. Jameson will have some registry or farrier info for us soon. Plus, we can still ask the sheriff and deputy about Lightning when we see them."

"You know, maybe Jax or Rufus has heard of Lightning," Rani said. "I say we go ask them right now before we help with dinner."

The kids were on their feet, heading for the stables, with Rani already out in front as usual. They found the two hired hands busy finishing the grooming and stabling of Bella, Zippy, and Mrs. Mayfield's horse for the night. The men looked up without stopping their work.

"Did you kids have a good ride?" Jax asked.

"Sure did" Lanny said, "and it sounds as if you guys had a good day with Cat and Lion. They've really gotten into the horses, I think."

"They're sweet kids, once you get past their tough exteriors," Jax replied. He finished securing Zippy in his stall. "But that's what we always seem to have to do with the saddle club kids. It's a shame. They're so young yet often so mixed up and tough as nails."

Lexi replied, "They haven't shared their stories with us yet, but I hope they will."

"Speaking of stories," Rani said, "have you guys heard about a white Arabian stallion?"

"What stallion is that?" Jax said. He stopped work and looked at Rufus, who paused then shook his head.

Moki replied, "Oh, just something we heard in Cody. It's not important."

"Beats me," Rufus said quickly with a shoulder shrug.

Both men went back to their stable tasks.

The kids stood there for a minute watching the men, hoping the two might remember something about the Arabian horse. But nothing more was said, so they turned to leave. Rani inhaled deeply before leaving, the smell of hay, alfalfa, and horses making her heart feel whole with promises of happy adventures.

But as the four started to head toward the bunkhouse to clean up, they heard a scream followed by a moan. It came from the back of the ranch house.

CHAPTER NINE

· ✧ ·

An Aunt and an Uncle

All the adults and kids came running. The detectives arrived on the scene right after Ben and Gracie, who had poked their heads out the back porch door from their kitchen duties.

There in the dust was an overturned bushel basket that had held a few dozen apples, now scattered around the area. And seated on the back stoop was a disgusted Aunt Maisie. She was rubbing her right ankle, which was already swelling.

"Well, doesn't that beat all," she said. Her pinched eyebrows showed her pain. "You'd think after all these years, I'd remember you have to step up to that stoop."

"Oh, Aunt Maisie," Mrs. Mayfield said. "Now, don't you worry." She turned to her husband. "Dear, can you help her up?"

"Of course. Could have happened to any of us," Mr. Mayfield said as he lifted Aunt Maisie off the ground effortlessly.

"Now, you all stop making such a fuss. Put me down this instant. I'll be fine in no time." The woman squirmed to be placed on her feet. Mr. Mayfield carefully accommodated her.

But as soon as Aunt Maisie's foot touched the ground, she let out another moan and started to collapse. Mr. Mayfield caught her before she could hit the ground again.

"Now, no more talk about being fine," Mrs. Mayfield said. "You're hurt. Can't you see your ankle is already swollen and discolored? And your knee is skinned."

"Oh, bother," the older woman said. "Of all times, right when dinner needs getting on the table."

"We have plenty of people to pitch in, don't we, kids?" Mr. Mayfield asked, looking to each face as he carried the woman through the back porch and into the kitchen to a chair offered by Gracie.

"Yes, sir!" everyone shouted in unison.

Without being asked, Catherine and Lionel started picking up apples and returning them to the basket. The detectives had followed the adults into the house. They set the table and helped with the cooking. Aunt Maisie looked on from the kitchen as she soaked her foot in a big pan of ice water and looked worriedly at her freshly bandaged knee.

Right on time at five o'clock, dinner was on the table. Lexi and Rani had even added candles and dimmed the lights, giving a formal feeling to the room. Aunt Maisie was carried to her place, and everyone was finally seated.

Catherine and Lionel said they had never eaten a meal by candlelight and glanced around at the silhouettes created by the twinkling flames. With his hands, Lionel started making some dog and bird shadow puppets that were cast on the dining room wall.

Catherine drew her hand up to her mouth. "It's beautiful and . . . *magical*."

"There are sure some cool uses for candles," Lionel added. "Tonight, they make me feel like a millionaire—like I'm eating in a fancy, expensive restaurant."

As was the dinner custom, each person in turn had to mention something they learned that day. Lionel shared that apples bruise easily. Catherine said horses were cool. Moki said he could tell it had been a while since he had ridden a horse. Gracie said Moki was a pirate when he wasn't being a detective. Once everyone had spoken and laughter subsided, platters and bowls were passed.

"I better be up and about by morning, or there won't be any breakfast," Aunt Maisie said shaking her head. She stared at the plate of food she'd hardly touched.

Mrs. Mayfield replied, "Oh no you don't. Walk on that foot too soon, and no dancing for you come party time Saturday night. We'll just all get up earlier and pitch in." Her worried look and tone of voice were not lost on Lanny.

"I have an idea," the boy said. "Let's call Uncle Rocky. I bet he'd come out and help in a flash."

Rocky Donovan, or "Uncle Rocky," as everyone called the gravelly-voiced man, was the Wyatt-Marlton family's friend, cook, and houseman. He and Dr. Wyatt were long-time friends, having met at one of Dr. Wyatt's archaeological excavation sites. Uncle Rocky had been employed by the twins' parents a few years before the two kids were born.

Aunt Maisie's fork stopped in midair. "A man? In my kitchen? No, thank you."

"But Uncle Rocky is the best chow jockey this side of the Rockies," Moki replied.

"And he's a sweet, charming teddy bear who always insists on a spotless kitchen after cooking," Lexi added. "You're gonna love him." She left out the part about him liking an occasional cigar.

It was settled. After dinner, Lanny called Uncle Rocky from the Mayfields' kitchen rotary-dial landline phone and presented him with the situation.

"Of course, I'll come out to the country," the man replied without hesitation. "In fact, I can arrive there tonight if you like, so you'll all have breakfast on the table in the morning. To be honest, it's been too quiet here on Quince Street with you kids gone. Your parents went to some museum doings up in Los Angeles. But Bruce is in and out, so he can take care of the pets." Uncle Rocky was referring to King Ramesses II, also known as Pharaoh, the family's energetic border collie, and Queen Cleopatra VII, nick-named Cleo, their prissy Abyssinian cat.

The Mayfield parents took turns on the phone thanking Uncle Rocky in advance for his help. Aunt Maisie even spoke with him briefly and was smiling by the time they finished talking. Lexi and Rani exchanged happy looks. Before the call ended, Moki asked to speak to Uncle Rocky.

"Hey, Uncle Rocky, this is Moki," the boy whispered with his hand cupped around the phone's mouthpiece. "Can you stop at a grocery store before you get here and pick up a few things? . . . Yeah, like all the ingredients for mac 'n' cheese. Oh, and some couscous. I need to give someone a major cooking lesson."

CHAPTER TEN

· ✧ ·

The Phantom Rides Again

By eight-thirty that evening, Uncle Rocky had arrived to help out following Aunt Maisie's sprained ankle and knee-scrape accident. He had two suitcases. One held his clothes. The other had an assortment of pots, pans, herbs and spices, his huge white apron with the saying, "That's How I Roll," across the top, and Moki's requested grocery items.

Aunt Maisie was in the living room easy chair with her foot wrapped and elevated. "Why, Uncle Rocky, I declare. You didn't need to bring those kitchen things. I have fully stocked cupboards as you'll soon discover. This may be the country, but we do know a thing or two about cooking out here," she huffed.

"I'm sure you do, Aunt Maisie, but you of all people will certainly understand that every great cook needs his— or her—favorite utensils for success," the tall, barrel-chested New Yorker said with a grin and a bow. "Now, would someone please show me to the kitchen?" But without waiting for a guide, Uncle Rocky picked up his suitcases and started making his way to the back of the house. The detectives smiled then followed him, already feeling that it had been a great idea to invite him to the ranch.

Helping unpack the kitchen items, Moki whispered to Uncle Rocky, "Thanks for the package of couscous. And on behalf of Rani, I also thank you for the mac 'n' cheese ingredients."

Mr. Mayfield had found an old but serviceable pair of crutches in the attic. In no time, Aunt Maisie came hobbling out to the kitchen. "Well, what do you think of my country kitchen, Uncle Rocky?"

"I think it's even better now, graced by your presence," he replied.

"Um, um, um. You surely are a charmer as Lexi said." She laughed as she found a chair and eased herself into it.

"But an honest one," Uncle Rocky said with a wink, taking her crutches and leaning them against a nearby wall within her reach. "I don't say it unless I mean it."

Everyone had joined them. Soon, however, Mr. and Mrs. Mayfield asked Catherine and Lionel, who seemed fascinated by a real live male cook, not one on a television show, to say their goodnights. It was time for bed, so they would be ready for a busy day of riding tomorrow. Both groaned a bit, but Uncle Rocky told them to hurry to bed so tomorrow morning would come faster. That's when they would get his famous breakfast surprise. The two were intrigued enough to obey and were soon on their way to the bunkhouse with the Mayfield parents following in their footsteps. Ben, Gracie, and the detectives were given permission to stay up a little while longer after agreeing to be in their cots no later than ten o'clock.

Moki watched the Mayfield parents and saddle club kids leave, then said, "Anybody up for a late night snack?"

Everyone was. Bowls, measuring utensils, and ingredients were quickly handed from cupboards as recipes were decided. Aunt Maisie cringed a little at the thought of her kitchen getting messy but soon relaxed. Rani and Lexi wanted to make mac 'n' cheese. And Gracie was hungry for her specialty, a mustard sandwich.

"A *what* kind of sandwich?" Moki asked as he pulled back and stared at the girl.

"Mustard, just mustard," Gracie replied. "Well, bread and butter, then mustard."

"Nothing else, just those three ingredients?" Moki asked.

Gracie nodded proudly and asked for his promise to try it. "And I bet Captain Jack Sparrow likes mustard sandwiches," she added with a twinkle in her large brown eyes.

"In the interest of culinary experimentation, and because I'm such a good pirate sport, I promise. Though I don't know if pirates have mustard handy in their ships' galleys."

"Sure they do," Rani said. "They find jars and jars of the stuff in treasure chests." She and Gracie snickered and high-fived.

"Yeah, Moki," Gracie added. "You know—little glass pots of gold!"

Moki groaned but knew he was licked. "Could knock a pirate dead that way," he said under his breath. But in a moment, he turned to the fun task ahead.

Lanny was content to assist as Moki taught Ben how to make a couscous salad.

Aunt Maisie and Uncle Rocky supervised as they sat back at the kitchen table and got better acquainted over some freshly brewed coffee and leftover apple pie.

By nine-thirty, Uncle Rocky and Aunt Maisie had said their goodnights and headed for their own rooms off the kitchen. The chefs had sampled each other's cooking, though, secretly, Moki had to add a slice of cheese to his piece of mustard sandwich from Gracie to make it edible. Ben devoured two helpings of the couscous salad and said he would be making it often. And the bowl of mac 'n' cheese had been scraped clean.

"Masks, be still now," Rani said, licking her lips.

As promised, the kids left the kitchen clean and spotless.

A few minutes before ten o'clock, the group headed for the back porch door, having decided to go to the bunk-house by way of the back yard. No sooner had Ben switched off the kitchen lights when the kids heard what sounded like a horse approaching from a distance. Approaching thunderously.

"That's the sound I heard before," Ben whispered, careful not to mention the Phantom Rider in front of Gracie. But it didn't matter now.

"Gracie, stop!" he shouted, reaching to keep her from

opening the screen door. It was too late. A huge white Arabian horse galloped across the yard toward the stoop.

Gracie screamed, "Oh Mama!"

Ben's courage—and anger—rallied. "Come on, you guys." He pushed past his startled sister and held the door open himself, followed quickly by the detectives and Gracie.

What a sight it was. Lightning was a beautiful but menacing horse. And on his back was the Phantom Rider! The rider reined in the horse, surprised to discover six onlookers so close. He was a big, burly man all in black leather from head to toe, who looked more foreboding in person than Ben could have ever possibly described. Within seconds, he had regained his composure. His eyes shone like sparks from the holes in his black ski mask.

He pulled on the reins and dug his spurs into the horse's side. That did the trick. The horse whinnied and reared up high as if to threaten the kids with his flailing front hooves.

Ben and Moki saw the danger and were the first to act. "Yah, yah!" they yelled. "Get away." They wanted to discover the Phantom's identity but not at the risk of all their lives, so they stayed huddled on the stoop.

It was everything the Phantom could do to sustain his control. But he was careful not to allow the kids to approach by putting a few yards' distance between himself and them. He turned Lightning in tight, dusty circles, so he could keep his eyes on the group. All the while, he never uttered a word.

Ben reached inside the porch door and flicked on the stoop's light. "It's my turn to shake my fist at you, dude," Ben shouted. "See this, Phantom? Now, get outta here!"

"I've got an idea," Moki said. In the confusion over Aunt Maisie's fall, the bushel basket of apples had not been carried indoors. There it sat on the back stoop. The boy reached in, picked up some apples, and began pelting the Phantom with them. The others quickly joined in.

"This one's for you, coward," Moki shouted. He threw the biggest apple he could find. It paid off as it hit the Phantom squarely in the back of the head with a thud.

"Good shot, bro," Lanny said, while keeping his eye on the Phantom.

Apples were now flying as courage grew. All the kids aimed high, trying to outdo Moki. Gracie unleashed all her excitement about being a junior detective with each throw. The group heard distinct "oofs" and "ows" from the rider as he was hit repeatedly, but he still said nothing else.

The excitement had awakened Uncle Rocky, Jax, and Rufus, who joined the scene, dressed in their boots and work pants over pajama tops. By now, horse and rider were many yards away but gave no sign of quitting their mission of terror. The cook, who always enjoyed being a part of the detectives' cases, picked up some apples and started throwing them, too. Though he aimed at the Phantom, one accidentally hit Lightning on his hindquarters. The spooked horse reared again, this time almost throwing his rider.

"Whoa, Lightning, whoa!" the Phantom shouted as he

struggled but managed to bring the horse under control.

Jax yelled, "Rufus, lasso that horse!"

The younger man, who had stood dazed, now ran to the barn for a rope. By the time he returned, however, Lightning and the Phantom Rider had sped away. All that remained were a veil of dust, the ground strewn with apples, and six kids doubled over with laughter. Rufus stood looking dumbfounded with the rope tangling limply from his hands.

"Well, now, what the heck was that?" Jax asked, puzzled by the kids' laughter. He scratched his head and watched horse and rider vanish into the distance in a growing dust cloud.

"Probably the person who's been stealing our ranch gear," Ben replied between chuckles.

"Too bad I couldn't have captured him or the horse," Rufus added. "I was too darn slow with the rope."

Lexi said, "Well, Uncle Rocky, you did super. You made the Phantom talk. But if only he had fallen off when you pegged the horse. We could have unmasked the guy on the spot. No lasso would have been needed, right Rani?"

Rani nodded between chuckles. "But please stop saying 'mask.'"

Lanny asked, "Ben, Gracie, did you recognize his voice?"

"No," they said in unison.

Then, Ben added, "But it did sound . . . kind of familiar."

"What in tarnation's going on out here, and why aren't

you kids in bed yet?" a groggy Aunt Maisie said. She had hobbled to the back door but had just missed all the excitement.

Ben suppressed another giggle and looked at her. "No good reason, Aunt Maisie. Just playing an on-horseback version of 'Bob for Apples' with a Phantom."

CHAPTER ELEVEN

· ✧ ·

A Rough Start

The six kids went to breakfast the next morning with a new plan: It was time to tell Ben's parents about the Phantom Rider. He was real. They knew that for sure now. Plus, the rider himself had confirmed the horse's name. They, therefore, had two important pieces of information to reveal.

But Mrs. Mayfield had already heard the news. "So, I understand Jax called the sheriff's office last night about the intruder," she said to her son, "but no one chose to tell your dad or me about it until this morning." Ben and Gracie recognized their mother's serious voice when they heard it. It was no use trying to tiptoe around the situation, let alone her.

Gracie started to speak, but Mom held up her hand. "Gracie, dear, let's have your brother explain."

Ben gave a deep sigh, but with downcast eyes, said, "You're right, Mom." He suddenly had no appetite despite

Uncle Rocky's breakfast surprise of banana-cinnamon waffles.

Now meeting his mother's gaze, the boy continued, "We *were* going to tell you at breakfast. And we figured, why wake you guys up when the sheriff or deputy couldn't get here until this morning, anyway?" He looked down again at the floor, knowing full well they weren't buying it.

"What your mother means, young man," Ben's dad said, "and I think you know it, is that we are the adults around here, and we need to know what's going on at all times—immediately. Jax said he didn't tell us because he figured you or Gracie would."

"Remember our family rule?" Mom added. "We share the good and the bad, no matter what. We're a team. We can't help if we aren't acquainted with your problems.

"Jax, Rufus, and Uncle Rocky have filled us in on the horse and rider," she continued, "so we won't rehash that in front of our guests. But we will talk more about this later. So now, let's all take a deep breath, refocus, and enjoy Uncle Rocky's fabulous meal to start a new day on a more positive note."

Breakfast was quieter than usual for everyone. Aunt Maisie tried to brighten moods by complimenting Uncle Rocky on the feast he had prepared, sharing that she was actually happy to have him around. Uncle Rocky smiled ear to ear. Lionel didn't help, however, when he added it was great that someone else was in trouble for a change besides him. Catherine got the conversation back on track by saying she was looking forward to another day riding Bella. Ben's appetite slowly returned as Mr. Mayfield asked the detectives what they had planned for the day.

Lanny replied, "After we talk with the sheriff or deputy about last night, I thought we could go explore your property. And if it's all right, I'd like to take the skeleton key and photograph with us that we found in Papa's treasure box. No telling what we might discover using them."

Mr. Mayfield instantly agreed to the plan.

Then Lexi took a deep breath and asked, "May Ben and Gracie go with us?" She was hoping the two Mayfield kids weren't getting grounded over the Phantom Rider secrets.

Mrs. Mayfield looked at her son's pleading eyes, then at Lexi. "Of course, he may," she said, the corners of her mouth curling up.

"Me, too, Mom?" Gracie asked with eyes bigger than her brother's.

"Yes, you too, Gracie." Mom smiled broadly and winked at her daughter.

"Thanks," Rani said with a twinkle in her eye directed at the young girl. "Our investigating wouldn't be as effective or as much fun without Gracie and Ben." Rani, Gracie, and Lexi each did a fist pump under the table.

Uncle Rocky stood to start clearing the buffet and asked, "Say, didn't I hear Jax mention there will be a cookout and campfire tonight for all you kids, including Cat and Lion?"

"That's right," Mr. Mayfield replied, happy for a reason to smile. "Our usual Wednesday night fun. You kids get to camp out overnight at the ranch's campgrounds not far from here. But all of you need to save a couple hours this afternoon to do some schoolwork."

The kids groaned simultaneously, and everyone laughed.

"That's cool about camping out," Lionel said. "Can we make s'mores? I've heard people talk about them, but I've never tasted them."

Rani replied, "It just so happens Lanny is the world's best s'mores maker."

"Then, s'mores it is for dessert tonight," Aunt Maisie said. "Uncle Rocky and I will be busy today preparing the food for you to take."

Uncle Rocky gave two thumbs up. "But you can only work sitting down," he added, assisting the woman with her crutches as she rose from the table.

"It's a deal, Uncle Rocky," she said.

Everyone was pleased by how well Aunt Maisie, usually very independent, had taken to being helped by her assistant cook.

Gracie pulled on her mom's shoulder and whispered, "I think Auntie Maisie's in love." The two giggled as everyone pushed their chairs back from the table.

Just then, the front doorbell rang. Mr. Mayfield admitted Deputy Buchanan to the living room. He apologized for coming instead of the sheriff. The head lawman was away handling an emergency.

The witnesses to last night's Phantom Rider episode each told what they had seen and provided descriptions of the rider and horse. Ben let it slip that last night wasn't the first time he had seen the Phantom. Instantly, he knew he was in trouble again. His parents' eyebrows raised, and Ben felt their stink eyes burning into the back of his head.

Ned Buchanan paused in his note-taking. "Do any of you have any idea who the person is?"

No one did.

Lanny had figured it was pointless to ask the deputy if he knew anything about Lightning since the man had been questioning them about the horse. The boy made a mental note to still check with the sheriff when they next met.

After a few more minutes of questioning, the deputy thanked the group and said he would start making inquiries into the matter. Mrs. Mayfield thanked him and showed him out. Then she turned without hesitation, her hand still on the doorknob, to face her son.

Ben dreaded seeing the lawman go. *Here it comes*, he thought, as he hung his head. He wished he could zap himself into invisibility as he pinched his eyes shut and grimaced.

The deputy had barely descended the first porch step when, right on cue, Dad began gruffly: "Ben, why didn't you tell us about the rider the first time you saw him?"

Ben slowly opened his eyes. The look on his father's face told him he was in serious trouble.

Ben paused, then faced his father. "I was too scared,

Dad. And I wanted to protect everyone from the crazy rider." He felt his face grow hot as his heart started to pound.

"Your gallantry was misplaced," Mom replied. "Until you're older, your dad and I are your knights in shining armor, not the other way around. Do I make myself clear, young man?"

Ben nodded and let out a big sigh of relief. He was glad the whole truth was out in the open now.

Mom continued with her hands on her hips. "Now, are there any more surprises or secrets we should know about before we get this day back on track?"

"That's it, Mom—really!" Ben replied with an attempt at a smile.

"Okay, then. Let's switch gears. Cat and Lion, you two follow me to the arena. The rest of you kids, have a great day exploring. Be careful, and be back here by three o'clock as usual, please."

Lionel smirked at Ben as he passed by and out the front door. Ben sighed deeply. He was now convinced that his sterling role-model image had instantly been tarnished, at least in Lionel's eyes. And if it had, he also knew that it was his own fault.

The six detectives turned to leave as well, but the landline phone in the living room rang. Ben picked it up. It was Dr. Jameson. They spoke all too briefly. Lanny immediately sensed the veterinarian had not found out anything that would help them identify the horse and rider.

Ben confirmed the bad news. "She said Lightning

doesn't appear to have been registered, and the local farrier hasn't worked on a white Arabian stallion for many years."

"Well, at least we now know we'll have to keep investigating about that," Lexi said with a shrug. She pushed past the others and out the front door while positioning her large straw western hat on her head.

Lanny gazed after her. His sister had some annoying habits, Lanny thought. But he also had to admit that she had a gift for optimistically seeing the big picture—beyond the present circumstances. He and the squad could always count on her for that.

CHAPTER TWELVE

· ✧ ·

Gold Mine Search

The kids shook off the disappointing news from Dr. Jameson and the rough start to the morning. They walked in the direction of the arena but peeled off to the bunkhouse. Lanny needed to get the key and photo from his knapsack to take with them. Jax and Rufus were already busy with Catherine and Lionel, so the six would have the barn to themselves. While they saddled their horses, they confirmed the day's mission—find Papa's gold mine "or bust." Soon, they were off with brighter spirits and can-do attitudes.

When they had ridden as far as the main gate to the ranch's access road, Rani asked Ben, "Can you point out your ranch's boundaries from here?"

Ben pointed upward and said that the Mayfields' acreage extended into the mountains to the west of them for a distance. The bulk of the ranch was comprised of meadows that hugged the eastern edge of those mountains and went north as far as they could see. From there, the ranch wrapped around that northern rim for a bit and dipped into the desert.

Moki rode up next to Ben. "Dude, how many acres is your ranch, anyway?"

"It's fairly small as Cody ranches go. Only about forty."

Lanny said, "Whoa! Forty acres? That's like . . . wait for it . . . thirty football fields! That may be small to you, but it's big to me when we're talking about exploring it. I suggest we form two teams and start searching."

Lexi, Rani, and Gracie teamed up, leaving the boys to group together. This worked well since each team would then contain a Mayfield expert in the local terrain.

Lanny reviewed out loud the notes from Rani's dad about how to find a possible gold mine by its contact rocks, any old ore car railroad tracks, and piles of boulders near a cave or mine entrance. He showed everyone the photo with the two young pine trees flanking the entrance to Papa's mine. They agreed to meet for lunch at a place Ben estimated would be about midpoint in the area to be covered. Gracie knew the spot. Lanny ended by reviewing safety precautions, including not entering a mine, as they had promised their parents in good faith.

"Just don't mention the 'S' word around Moki," Lexi pretend-whispered.

"Oh, you mean 'snake'?" Rani blurted. The two girls started laughing.

"I heard that," Moki said. "Snakes—as well as girls—bring *nui ka pilikia*."

Lexi translated for Gracie, "He means 'lots of trouble.'"

Gracie was intrigued by the island language. "Moki, I'll pay you in mustard sandwiches for Hawaiian lessons. Do pirates speak Hawaiian?"

But all Moki said under his breath was, "Ooh, more *pilikia*." Without another word, he prompted Grandma to canter, so he could join the boys and put some distance between himself, Gracie, and her mustard threat.

By lunchtime, the two exhausted, hungry groups met to discuss their findings as they ate. Unfortunately, neither had found a cave, let alone a gold mine. Moki was happy to report no snake run-ins. As they were finishing the last of the food, they decided to continue searching as far north as possible before they had to meet to return to the ranch.

Lanny said to the others, "I'm getting worried. It's Wednesday already. The week will be over before we know it, and we've made little progress on our case."

Lexi, ever positive, replied, "Well, we do know Lightning's name for sure. And the Phantom Rider knows we're on to him."

"Which could put us in more danger," Rani said. "We'll need to be extra careful."

"Good point, bestie girlfriend," Lexi replied. She

leaned over to squeeze Rani's forearm with both hands.

Rani stared at her aching arm. "BFF!"

Lexi got the message and let go with a sincere apology.

Moki said, "Back to the Phantom. His knowing about us could work in our favor. Maybe we've spooked him enough so that he'll start taking foolish chances."

"Let's hope so, dude," Ben said. "You know, I'm glad the Phantom business is no longer a secret from my parents and my sister. It's a weight off my shoulders, and the police are helping now. Plus, it was fun last night with all of you there helping me take on that dude. When I think about how freaked I was the first time I saw him from my bedroom window—"

"That's what friends—and family—are for," Lanny replied. "Lexi and I would be in major trouble if we kept big secrets from our parents."

"Could've shared it with me," Gracie said to Ben with a pout. "I wouldn't have told."

Ben looked sideways at his sister and smirked.

When the last of the lunch was eaten and the trash packed for home, the group rode out to finish exploring the area going north. The same teams split off again.

After the boys had traveled a ways, Ben said, "Hey, guys, come check this out." He had slid off Jet and slowly walked a short distance toward some brush. Lanny jumped off Sam, hoping Ben had found the entrance to Papa's gold mine or at least some gold-bearing ore. No such luck.

"I think it's a rattlesnake den in an old rabbit warren,"

Ben said. "Yup, here are some rattlesnake droppings at the entrance. Rattlesnakes like to keep their dens clean, so they push the waste out."

Moki stayed on his mount. "Oh, great. First a snake den with possible fangs of death. Then snake poop. Count me out. Ben, maybe you can find a new friend—like Lanny!—who can get behind your weird reptilian interests." He shuddered knowing snakes were nearby. The three boys exchanged grins.

Lanny was, indeed, interested and spent a moment looking. "Cool, Ben, but time's flying. We need to get back to searching for the mine."

Ben agreed and remounted Jet. Moki was happy to put some distance between himself and the den of doom.

Meanwhile, the girls' team had focused on the rocks and trees defining the hillside.

"Darn. I'm seeing lots of granite, but no connecting schist," Rani said from atop Ginger.

Lexi replied, "Toby led me to some white quartz over here, but not the dirty, gold-speckled quartz your dad described, Rani. And no ore car railroad tracks or twin pine trees. Wish I felt as happy as the chirping birds seem to be. But we'll figure it out. Yes, we'll figure it out." She sounded as if she was trying to convince herself.

"I know it's around here somewhere," Gracie said. She slumped in her saddle. "Cookie, don't you know?" The horse looked back at Gracie, then forward again, as if shaking her head no. Gracie chuckled and patted the horse's neck.

At a quarter to three, the two groups met back at the lunch spot with their sad reports. "Well, I guess today was a bust after all," Moki said.

The others slowly nodded.

They turned their horses for home. Lanny rode in silence. There was so much left to do in a short amount of time. He wanted to explore the treacherous northern rim of the property somehow. Lexi read her twin's mind.

"Lanny, we'll get the job done. We always do. Plus, now we know where not to look. Let's focus on the fun we'll have camping out tonight."

The boy cracked a wry smile at his still optimistic sister and cantered ahead.

CHAPTER THIRTEEN

· ✧ ·

Meow!

At three o'clock, the six defeated explorers reached the ranch. They watered, groomed, and stabled their horses, then headed for the bunkhouse to clean up before lesson time.

Catherine and Lionel were already busy on their schoolwork with Mrs. Mayfield as tutor. Lanny sighed heavily as he put the skeleton key and photo away in his large knapsack and yanked the zipper closed with a zing. *Tomorrow, we will use these again, but with better luck*, he told himself to cheer up.

Two hours flew by with Bruce's fun virtual Zoom lessons about panning for gold in 1849. There was even some fascinating information about a few of the most dangerous outlaws Papa Mayfield had captured and turned in. Gracie enjoyed learning from the materials, as she had hoped. How thrilling that her own relative was a famous historical figure! A short time later, math pages were also finished, and books could be closed. Yay! It was time to prepare for the evening's campout.

The eight kids each packed a small knapsack for the night, following Mrs. Mayfield's strict guidelines. Jax and Rufus usually accompanied the saddle club kids on the campouts, but since there were so few kids this week, Mrs. Mayfield had asked Uncle Rocky if he wanted to go as lone chaperone instead. The cook had agreed wholeheartedly. Jax and Rufus thanked him and Mrs. Mayfield for the night off.

All the kids helped pack the huge basket of food and boxes of camping gear into the van. Everyone was especially anxious to get to the campgrounds. But Lionel was suddenly anxious for a different reason. He had forgotten something and wanted to make a quick trip back to the bunkhouse to get it.

"What did you forget?" Mrs. Mayfield asked.

Lionel pulled on her shoulder until her ear was level with his mouth. "Uh, my . . . stuffed lion toy . . . you know . . . to sleep with," he whispered. Then, he glanced around, hoping no one else had heard. "Please let me go get it. I'll be fast."

Mrs. Mayfield slowly smiled at this request and replied, "Well, all right. Hurry up, then. Time's a wasting. I'll give you one minute and no more before sending someone to bring you back." Lionel's eyes lit up. She watched him race off, surprised that he had managed to keep his secret from the other boys so far.

Lionel had it all worked out. Once he retrieved his toy,

he planned to tuck it inside his shirt, so the other kids, especially Catherine, couldn't possibly tease him about still sleeping with a stuffed animal. He had been hiding it under his blankets all week.

Lionel made it to the bunkhouse in record time. "Phew! It's hot in here," he said out loud once he was inside. The room was, indeed, warm and stuffy from the mid-afternoon desert heat that had settled in the sleeping quarters. Instead of flipping on the air conditioner for such a quick visit, he ran over and opened the back door. He stood on the threshold for a few seconds to let the cooler air rush over himself while gazing dreamily out into the gathering dusk.

Remembering his mission and its time limit, he turned and ran to the closet. There was his small suitcase on the floor. He stooped and yanked it out by the handle to get the toy from inside where he had hidden it each morning. Kneeling on the floor, he pushed on the golden lock flaps. But try as he might, they wouldn't budge.

"Come on!" he shouted at the flaps. "Hey. Somebody must have locked my suitcase. Grr!" He had to figure out something fast to preserve his secret. One of the adults or kids might show up if he took too much longer.

Right at that second, however, a new problem loomed that would make his suitcase issue minor in comparison. A distinct panting sound caused Lion to look up immediately. "What the—?" he started to say as he quickly turned to see its source.

To his horror, about ten feet away, swaying side to side, padded a six-foot long mountain lioness! Her golden eyes looked around cautiously as she huffed more loudly. The cat had obviously come in through the open back door and seemed just as surprised to see Lionel as he was to see her. She paused for a few seconds, perhaps trying to determine her direction. She chose and was now heading right for him.

"Oh Mama!" The boy stood slowly, backed up, and almost toppled over as he hit the edge of a cot. He stood up again and faced the tawny-colored cat. Hot surges passed through his body, and he could hear his heart thumping against his ribcage. *Dude, just don't pass out now*, he told himself.

Many more thoughts raced like lightning through Lionel's head. First, he didn't want to be another lion's dinner. And he was angry at himself for breaking the ranch rule about not inviting wildlife indoors by leaving a door open. Most important, he wondered desperately what he could do to save himself.

Lionel noticed that the panting animal had humongous paws and long, sharp claws that scritch-scratched with each step. As the cat kept approaching, beads of perspiration erupted on the boy's forehead. He felt his teeth chattering uncontrollably from mounting terror. Suddenly, somehow, everything shifted into slow motion as he watched the cat inch closer and closer. Lionel tried to turn to run, but as much as he willed himself to do so, his feet wouldn't obey.

He discovered that he couldn't shout. His voice had vanished. Was he in a trance? Had the animal hypnotized him?

It felt to the boy as if an hour had passed when he heard someone gasp, then start shouting from the front door, "Yah, yah, get out of here!" *Thank goodness*! "Lion, it's Ben. Get behind me very slowly. Just don't crouch down."

Mrs. Mayfield had sent her son to see what was taking Lionel so long. But the younger boy's feet remained glued to the floor with his heart pounding as the wild animal continued to come closer. Like being in a nightmare, no words came out when he tried to shout to Ben.

Ben sized up the situation and knew he had to act fast. He calmly stepped in front of the terrified boy and sucked in his breath so as to stand as tall as he could. Then, he made eye contact with the animal and began waving his arms slowly and shouting at the intruder again. "Get out of here! We don't want you here. Go home. Get!"

But, rather than retreat, the mountain lioness started to crouch. Her huffing changed to a throaty growl. Ben knew she was hungry and preparing to pounce. He had to do something drastic if they were to survive, but experience told him it wasn't wise to take his eyes off the lioness or make any quick movements.

Just when Ben thought he and Lionel would be history, someone else had come into the room. That someone was now standing right behind him. Without turning around to see who it was, Ben said, "Hand me those hiking sticks," pointing to his right. He hoped the person would be brave and do what he asked.

Slowly, the helper bent sideways and lifted the sticks from where they rested against the wall, inching them toward Ben, and using them to tap his right hand softly. He wasted no time pulling the sticks upright into an X-shape. He banged them together to make as much noise as he could. He doubled down on his shouting, joined by the hidden helper.

The mountain lioness backed up, looking for a way to retreat. Finding it, she took off out the back door at a run. Ben ran, too—toward the door, slamming it shut and sliding the bolt lock into place. "Whew! That was too close for comfort," he said as he wiped rivers of perspiration from his forehead. He looked up to find the helper was Catherine!

Ben smiled at her, then turned toward Lionel, who was still in a trance. But Catherine was already there, hugging the boy and telling him to snap out of it, that everything was all right, and that he was safe now.

Lionel's eyes slowly refocused. His stiff body relaxed so much that his legs gave out. Ben caught him before he could hit the floor and eased him down to sit on the cot.

Lionel wavered a bit, blinked, and realized he was looking at Ben and Catherine. Jumping to his feet, he shouted at them, "Watch out! There's a lion in here."

Ben put his hand on the boy's shoulder and pushed him back to a sitting position. "Relax, dude. It's over," Ben said. "You're the only Lion in here now."

"Cat?" Lion said, still not grasping the entire situation. "What're you doing in the boy's bunkhouse? You aren't supposed to be in here."

"Hey, dude," Ben said. "Be happy she is here. She just saved our lives."

"Wow," Lionel said once the three had rejoined the other campers and adults, and everyone had heard the scary tale. "Cat, you're something else," he said. "I'll never think girls are weaklings again. Thanks for keeping us from being eaten. Can you imagine what my friends would say if I had been? They'd laugh and say, 'Looks like one lion ate another lion.' Guess I'm no ferocious lion after all. Just a little, puny scaredy cat." He stared down at his sneakers.

"You're welcome, Lion," Catherine said. "And even the bravest person in the world would be afraid if they came face to face with a wild animal. Heck, I *was* 'a scaredy cat.' But Ben's the real hero here. He did most of the work scaring off *that* cat."

Ben shook his head. "Thank goodness you showed up when you did, Cat. And, Lion, mountain lions attack when they think their prey's weak. You weren't attacked, so that lioness must have sensed your strength."

"Yeah, okay. Thanks, Ben. But how did you know what to do, dude?" Lionel asked.

"Been there myself when I left a door open—once and only once. Fortunately, my dad had taught me what to do, like 'get big, get loud.' And it's probably a good thing that you froze and didn't try to bolt. Nothing wild animals like better than prey on the run. *Fun and games before mealtime,* they must think." Ben smiled, knowing how far Lionel and Catherine had come, and that his own position as a positive role model was back in force for the saddle club kids.

"Best training ever," Lionel replied. "Thank you, Mr. Mayfield, for teaching Ben what to do." Lionel looked up at the man with soft eyes and a huge smile.

Mr. Mayfield grasped Lionel's shoulder, shook it gently, and said, "I could begin a long lecture right now, but I think you've learned your lesson the hard way, Lion. And that's often the best kind of learning because it sticks with you."

He turned to Mrs. Mayfield and said, "I'll call the park ranger later tonight and report the incident. Oh, and I'll let our friends Jed and Emma Hollister know. Since they own the ranch next door, they'll especially need to be on the lookout for that lioness."

Mr. Mayfield turned back to the kids. "But for now, enough said—except, come on. Let's get you eight adventurers to the campgrounds."

CHAPTER FOURTEEN

· ✧ ·

By the Light of the Campfire

Lionel, Ben, and Catherine were safe following the mountain lion scare, and everyone was anxious to begin the fun night. The four detectives congratulated Ben and Catherine on their extraordinary bravery and reassured Lionel that he was no chicken.

Uncle Rocky and all the kids except Ben piled into the van. Mr. Mayfield was behind the wheel since, by law, Uncle Rocky wasn't allowed to drive the saddle club kids. Ben would follow on Jet so there would be transportation back to the ranch in case of an emergency. Uncle Rocky had on his fancy cowboy boots and Stetson western hat that seemed hilarious back in Las Palmitas but very appropriate tonight. They waved good-bye to Mrs. Mayfield, and to Aunt Maisie, who had hobbled out to the front porch to wish them a fun time. She gave Uncle Rocky a special wave, which he returned. Gracie, Lexi, and Rani hadn't missed the two adults' mutual attraction. The three girls snickered softly.

The campgrounds were a little over a mile from the ranch house. Lanny was pleased to discover they were heading north where he still wanted to explore. Looking to his left out the window, he could see the northwestern mountainous rim of the property. The campgrounds were on a flatter portion of land, which was a mix of meadow and the edge of the desert. The mountains and desert looked more spectacular from here than from the ranch house.

As the van sped along, a more relaxed Lionel retold in detail the parts of the story that he could remember about his dangerous mountain lioness encounter.

Soon, the car pulled over, and everyone spilled out. Mr. Mayfield had been there earlier setting up the two tents. Nearby were an outhouse, a water spigot, two picnic tables, a sizable pile of firewood, and a large campfire pit ringed with stones. There was even a small stable for Jet next to the tents.

"When do we get to make s'mores?" Lionel asked the second he got out of the van.

"After dinner," Uncle Rocky replied. "And you won't be sorry to wait when you see what Aunt Maisie and I have packed for chowtime."

Lanny pulled his bag from the van and added, "Besides, Lion, s'mores taste better when you make them in the dark over a roaring campfire. We still have an hour of daylight left."

Mr. Mayfield called out, "Food later. First, everyone, start helping to unload this van." The kids were snapped back to reality and the task at hand.

The girls won the coin toss and got to choose their tent first. They took the one next to Jet's stable. In no time, all the gear, food, and personal belongings were stowed. Mr. Mayfield reviewed the rules with the group, got in the van, and drove away, not to return barring an emergency until nine o'clock the next morning.

Meanwhile, Ben led Jet to his little stable. He brushed and fed his horse and covered him with a new woolen blanket. The Phantom Rider or someone else had stolen the original from the barn last month.

Lanny and Moki helped Lionel roll out his sleeping pad and sleeping bag inside their spacious tent. Lexi, Rani, and Catherine were getting settled in next door as well.

Gracie was outside helping Uncle Rocky organize the cooking utensils and start a blazing campfire. Shortly, its crackling sound and woodsy aroma promising adventure and food beckoned the other kids back outside.

Everyone was soon huddled around the campfire. Night was coming on and with it a sudden drop in temperature. Rani inhaled deeply. "Nothing like the scents of a campfire and desert sage to bring on an appetite."

Moki nodded. "I don't usually need any help with my appetite, but, sure, I can get behind that idea."

"Whoa, check out the moon." Lexi pointed to the northeast. A huge, almost full yellow-orange moon was rising over the desert. The night chorus of hissing crickets, hooting great horned owls, bats zipping through the air, and coyotes calling was just beginning.

As darkness deepened, Lionel added, "Wow. Look at the stars. There are millions of 'em. Never seen so many back home."

The detectives named some constellations for him and Catherine.

From the campfire, the sound of a big pot of bubbling cowboy beans soon drew everyone's attention. Uncle Rocky handed each person a wire stick with a hotdog attached and said, "Okay, time for a hot dog roast." No more coaxing was needed. Everyone started roasting while Uncle Rocky set out plates, hotdog buns, carrot and celery sticks, and all the fixings for the dogs.

"Hey, Gracie," Moki said. "Here's where your mustard sandwich would come in handy. Wrapped around a hotdog." His laughter echoed off the mountains.

Gracie frowned. "Then, it wouldn't be a true mustard sandwich. Hmph!"

"Don't forget these," Uncle Rocky added. From the campfire, he pulled out hot foil pouches filled with steaming potato slices, onion rings, and bell pepper chunks steeped in melted butter. "I call 'em Hobo Potatoes."

Within a short time, the campers had eaten the last of the hotdogs, licked potato remnants from the foil pouches, and scraped the bottom of the bean pot.

Lionel said, "Boy, oh boy! Food sure tastes different outdoors."

"I think it tastes best out under the stars," Catherine replied and smiled.

"Yeah, that's not a sensation you can get from eating microwaved pizza pockets at the kitchen table," Uncle Rocky said.

"No, siree!" Lionel replied with a major shake of his head. "But, now, what about the s'mores?"

"Don't you want your big dinner to settle first?" asked Uncle Rocky.

Lionel eyed him and said, "I'll *settle* for some s'mores—now . . . I mean, please."

Uncle Rocky smiled. "That's more like it, Lion. Thanks for remembering the magic word."

Lanny took his cue and got out the ingredients and equipment. "Okay, Cat and Lion. Here's my recipe. Start by putting some chocolate candy bar pieces on top of one graham cracker square." That was done. "Next, toast two marshmallows on a stick." The sticks used for the hotdogs were quickly brought back into service until the marshmallows were warm and gooey. "Okay, now, place your marshmallows on top of the chocolate pieces. Then, press the second cracker square down over that. Put your masterpiece into your magic, handy-dandy s'mores grill basket, and hold it over the fire until the chocolate starts to melt. Don't forget to toast the crackers on both sides quickly, so you don't burn them. That's all there is to it."

With a little help from the older kids and Gracie, Catherine and Lionel were successful on their first try. The saddle club kids' pride in their accomplishments was obvious as they licked the chocolate and marshmallow goo from their fingers. Many more s'mores were toasted. Soon, everyone had their fill.

Lionel rubbed his belly and smiled. "That was the best dinner and dessert I ever ate."

"Me, too," Catherine replied. She yawned and stretched as the campfire mesmerized her.

Then, everyone helped clean up and stow the gear, food, and trash in airtight containers so as not to attract wild animals. Lionel and Moki each made a point of requesting no mountain lioness or snake visitors.

Afterwards, the group huddled around the campfire again. Lionel made more hand shadow puppets, which he taught the others how to do. Uncle Rocky started a cycle of ghost stories. Ben and Gracie told a few they had heard Jax and Rufus share when those two men chaperoned the campers. Then, Lexi led everyone in her favorite campfire song, "On Top of Spaghetti," as they swayed side to side to the beat. This cheered up Catherine, who had gotten a bit frightened by the spooky stories.

Lanny shared a superstition about cowboy and cowgirl hats. "Never place your hat on a bed. It invites bad luck or an argument. Or worse . . ." He paused for dramatic effect, checking that he had Catherine's and Lionel's full attention. "It might even predict injury or . . . death! That's because it's believed that all the good luck can run out of the hat when it's placed brim-side-down on a surface. Also, a hat on a bed might signal that the wearer has died."

"I know a few," Moki said. All eyes were on him. "If

you compete in a rodeo, remove any money from your pocket first. Otherwise, that's all you might win that day. Plus, don't eat chicken before an event, or you might become what you eat. Never wear yellow in the arena. It's bad luck because some people think the color represents cowardice. And cowgirls often wear a different color sock on each foot for good luck."

Rani added, "Did you know that horseshoes are good luck symbols? They were made of iron, *and* iron was believed to keep away evil spirits. And always hang a horseshoe with the heel points up, or all the good luck will drain out of it."

"Whoa!" was all Catherine and Lionel could say.

All too soon, Uncle Rocky stood up, stretched and yawned, and announced it was time for bed. Gracie wanted to stay up longer but, being a good sport, she went with Catherine to the tent so the girl wouldn't be alone. A short time later, no sounds were heard from their shelter. Ben and Uncle Rocky helped Lionel get tucked in for the night. Ben rejoined the four detectives outside a short time later once Uncle Rocky was snoring at the back of the boys' tent. The boy was glad to have some sister-free time with his friends.

The five teens sat in silence savoring the nighttime, each other's company, and the dwindling glow of the campfire. The waxing gibbous moon had risen high over the desert. Quiet blanketed the land with only an occasional mournful call from a distant coyote or a wide-awake red-tailed hawk's screech. Sleepiness was beginning to overtake them one by one.

Unexpectedly, Lanny jumped to his feet. "Ben, *what's that*?" He pointed high up into the mountains that formed the northwestern edge of the Mayfields' ranch property. Indeed, a dim glow seemed to be emanating from somewhere behind one of the outcroppings.

"Beats me," Ben said. "There's nothing up there except rocks and trees."

"Maybe someone's camping out up there," Lexi said, now on her feet.

"Or maybe someone's lost, and that's an enormous flashlight," Rani offered.

"Whoever it is, they're trespassing on Mayfield property," Moki replied.

Ben nodded. "I've got an idea. What if two of us ride Jet and see how close we can get to the source?"

It was decided Lexi would go with Ben. Maybe one boy wouldn't be missed from the tent if Uncle Rocky or Lionel woke up, but two probably would. Lexi and Ben tiptoed to Jet's little stable while Rani, Moki, and Lanny went to their tents. They wanted to be awakened when the two investigators returned. Lexi and Ben said they would if anything interesting was discovered.

Ben quietly saddled Jet while Lexi looked on. Then, he walked the horse well out of camp to maintain quiet before the two mounted. Lexi held on from behind Ben. They rode for a few minutes until they could get as good a view as possible of the area where the light still appeared. Because of the nature of the mountainous terrain, the only thing they could make out was the light Lanny had seen, but much brighter now.

"I don't have a clue what's going on up there," Ben said. "And it's too dangerous riding into those mountains in the dark by ourselves to find out. I'd be grounded for life if I did. This is as far as we can go tonight."

"We'll have to head up there in the morning after all of us can get our horses from the ranch," Lexi replied. "Lanny did want to explore that area. And, anyway, daylight will help."

The two sat and watched for a few more minutes.

Soon, the mysterious light abruptly disappeared, and the landscape was still. Ben was about to turn Jet around to head back to the campsite. Within seconds, however, he and Lexi heard the distinct sound of pounding horse's hooves descending from the once-lit area, but from the far northern side. In less than a minute, a pale flash was seen. Both Ben and Lexi shivered. There was no mistaking it. A white animal was clearly visible, bathed in moonlight. Lightning! He—and probably the Phantom Rider—were racing at breakneck speed northeast across the wind-worn desert.

CHAPTER FIFTEEN

· ✧ ·

A Colorful Ghost Town

The smell of sizzling bacon roused the campers bright and early the next day. Lexi and Ben had jointly decided not to awaken their tentmates the night before after returning from their investigation of the mysterious glowing light on the mountain since little had been learned. They crawled out of their cozy tents, still a bit groggy from their extra-late night.

Uncle Rocky was standing, beating pancake batter in a large bowl. The other sleepyheads were slowly emerging from their tents. Catherine and Lionel had already dressed and joined the cook, anxious to see what he was preparing as they warmed themselves by the new campfire. The two had fun taking turns running to and from the woodpile to stoke the flames. Sitting around the nearby picnic table, Lexi and Ben filled in the other four about their late-night journey.

"No question now," Lanny said. "We're heading for that outcropping later this morning."

"Yeah, we need to know why the Phantom and Lightning were up there on that mountain," Moki replied.

"And why the area was lit up like a Christmas tree," Gracie added with big eyes.

"And where the Phantom went at an insane speed afterwards," Rani said.

"Agreed," Lanny said. "And let's hope it *was* Lightning and the Phantom. Anyway, it's now Thursday. No time to lose. With any luck, another busy day ahead."

Uncle Rocky turned from flipping flapjacks and called to the group, "Hey, no freeloaders allowed at this campground. You kids want breakfast? You better get over here and help."

The six detectives needed no more prompting since their bellies were growling, and the food smelled especially good in the crisp morning air. Lexi noticed what a difference a brilliant sunrise and some chirping birds could make to dispel the dread that had overtaken her following last night's Phantom sighting. But now to the food and a new day. In no time, she and the others had set the table and were laughing and gobbling down generous helpings of Uncle Rocky's blueberry pancakes, bacon, and fried eggs.

"Okay, campers. Better get a move on with the cleanup and packing," the cook announced after the meal. "It's twenty minutes to nine already. Mr. Mayfield will be here shortly to take us back to the ranch."

Time had indeed flown. The kids discussed how much fun they had had as they licked maple syrup from their fingers, repacked, and took down the tents. Uncle Rocky finished the dishes and doused and stirred the campfire until he was certain no embers remained.

At precisely nine o'clock, the Mayfields' van pulled into the campgrounds. Both Mayfield parents got out and trotted toward the campers. They were inundated first by the two jubilant saddle club kids, who had trouble taking turns describing their cool camping adventures.

Lionel roared more loudly than Catherine and won out. "The s'mores were dee-licious," he said, "and Uncle Rocky's quite the dude for an old guy. He knows some way scary campfire stories and wants to teach us how to play a card game called Texas hold 'em back at the ranch."

Uncle Rocky wagged his finger and was quick to add, "True, but no betting allowed, kids."

Mrs. Mayfield replied, "Hmm . . . well, I guess it would be all right." She smiled, then laughed as Lionel and Catherine continued to hug her.

"Sleeping in a tent was fun," Catherine was finally able to report. "No animals got in, and I didn't have any nightmares. And I didn't put my hat on my bed, because it's bad luck. Can we have s'mores at the Halloween party Saturday night?"

Catherine's last comment reminded Lanny how soon the week would end and how much more work they had to do if they were going to solve their case by then. He was relieved once everything was packed into the van, so they could get back to the ranch for their horses and begin investigating the strange occurrences on the mountain ridge.

In a short time, the van crawled up the ranch driveway. Jax and Rufus waved their greetings from near the barn. Aunt Maisie raised a crutch as her hello from the front porch.

Once Uncle Rocky got out of the car, he said, "Now, Aunt Maisie, you stay off that foot for two more days, so you'll be fit as a fiddle for all the dancing we're gonna do at the party."

"Foot's better, thanks," she replied, beaming. "Knee, too. And you've got yourself a deal, partner, come Saturday night."

Everyone grabbed some items from the van, and soon the unpacking was finished. Catherine, Lionel, and Mrs. Mayfield proceeded to the barn. They would begin the day by learning how to groom and saddle their horses.

Ben had decided last night he would be more forthcoming with his parents if he had a problem. So, he pulled his dad aside and told him about the strange lights on the remote area of their property he and Lexi had seen, about Lightning and, very likely, the Phantom Rider.

"Thanks, son. I appreciate your honesty. And I know how much Lanny wants to investigate the northern area." He turned to the boy. "Unfortunately, there's going to be a rainstorm today, so it won't be safe for anyone to travel up into those rugged mountains right now." He heard Lanny groan. "Don't worry, Lanny. Tomorrow's predicted to be sunny. I know that search is important for the case. But the mountain trails will be slick and dangerous. I'll call the sheriff's office today and report possible trespassers up there."

"I suspect that search will be important," Lanny said. "We'll definitely need to go up there tomorrow. In the meantime, we have another lead to follow up, northeast of here."

"That sounds like Rainbow Flats," Mr. Mayfield replied.

The kids nodded.

Lanny looked at Mr. Mayfield sideways, hoping their ghost town visit wouldn't be overruled.

"Okay, the terrain is flat, but be careful. Stay together. As far as I know, that old town is deserted, so watch out for wild animals possibly holed up there. And Ben, please take care of your sister."

Gracie sighed and replied, "Uh, Dad. I'll be the one looking after him."

Ben frowned. "Hmph!"

"Then, all of you—look out for one another. I know you're in a rush, but take it easy."

Lanny turned to the other five. His glum face showed his disappointment about the pace though he was happy they could still explore.

Moki knew the look well. "Let's get to our horses *wiki-wiki* and chase some ghost town ghosts, bro."

Lanny replied, "Yes, as quickly as possible. Darn, the skeleton key and gold mine photo will have to wait in the bunkhouse until tomorrow. But now, let's make tracks for Rainbow Flats."

Lexi said, "Nice little rhyme, brother," and gave him two thumbs up and a smile.

The six riders were soon retracing the route they had traveled by car, passing near the campgrounds, and finally branching off from that trail to head farther northeast across the desert. Serious storm clouds were creeping in like dark gray scowling monsters. A brisk, cool wind was already whipping up some nearby tumbleweeds. The weather conditions spurred the horses and riders forward.

Rani was riding next to Moki. "Hey, Moki. Better watch where you step in Rainbow Flats. The place is probably crawling with snakes."

She and Lexi exchanged glances and smirks.

"No need to remind me, but *mahalo*, anyway," he said, trying not to look nervous.

"You're welcome," she replied. She and Lexi rode off laughing.

"Girls and snakes—*nui ka pilikia*," he muttered and patted his horse's neck. "I'm sticking with you, little but mighty Grandma."

The rain was holding off, but the wind had picked up even more. Dust devils started swirling amidst the cacti, kicking up sand in the distance. To relieve her sense of desolation, Rani called out, "Hey, Ben. How did Rainbow Flats get its name?"

Ben replied, "I've heard it told that the founder of the

town named it Rainbow Flats because when he was riding across the desert during a storm, he looked up and noticed a rainbow. He supposedly followed it to its end, and that's where he established the town."

Gracie added, "And the land was flat, so that's where the 'Flats' part came from."

The rest of the group rode on in silence. Within an hour, the faint outlines of structures in ruins became visible. What had once been a serviceable trail into Rainbow Flats was now blanketed with sagebrush and tumbleweeds. Rani spotted a roadrunner scurrying out of their way. No telling what might be hiding in the tall grasses and overgrown bushes that flanked their route. She was glad they rode horses and didn't have to walk. Nature's sounds had replaced all those of the once-bustling community that must have inhabited the town over a hundred years ago.

The first few buildings the kids approached were nearly unrecognizable sheets of rotted wood, now housing squawking crows flying in and out where windows had once existed. If the birds were calling for food scraps from people, they were out of luck. Battered wooden boardwalks fronted small Victorian cottages and false-front shops on both sides of Main Street. A sign over one building said, "Seymour Adams, M.D." It dangled from a solitary hook and was eerily squeaking in the dusty wind. The occasional haunting sound of a muffled bell goaded the visitors as the winds danced through the steeple of the town's dilapidated church in the distance.

"This place gives me the creeps," Moki said as he hunkered down in his saddle.

"No kidding, bro," Lanny replied. "But what a perfect setting for an old Western movie."

Lanny pointed to the first building on their right, which looked like a rickety old barn. He could picture cowboys, cowgirls, and miners riding into town and bedding down their animals there before heading for the saloon, shops, or hotel. "Just in case we aren't alone, I think we should tie up our horses in that barn. No sense in tipping off someone who might be hiding here—if anyone really is—that we're around."

Everyone followed Lanny in single file. Lexi and Gracie slid off their horses first and tackled the job of opening one of the barn's double doors. Surprisingly, it opened almost effortlessly. The six kids walked their horses inside. All were happy finally to be out of the wind although chilly drafts still stubbornly pushed through the decrepit, wooden slats, causing a faint whistling sound.

The group quickly surveyed the inside of what had been a livery stable and found a central work area with an ice-cold forge and anvil where a blacksmith had once pounded horseshoes and other ironware. Antique pots and chains still hung overhead. They had their pick of some empty stalls that formed the perimeter of the interior.

"Look, Rani," Gracie said, pointing to a couple of stalls. "Those horseshoes are nailed up the correct way. We'll have good luck." The two gave a thumbs up.

Rani felt they needed good luck in this drafty old barn. Her usual impressions of having a whole heart and happy adventures in barns were rapidly being replaced by something more sinister. She now pictured a hole in her heart and the threat of dark adventures awaiting all of them. She hoped she was wrong—unless, of course, it was in service to their solving the mystery.

Ben and his horse were in front of the others, so they ambled to one of the back stalls. Just as the boy was leading Jet into one of them, both stopped abruptly. "Uh, guys. Come check this out."

The others quickly joined Ben. They stood gazing at an excess of modern horse gear. But no horse. A large bucket still holding well water was at the back of the stall, along with a shorter, round bucket containing some alfalfa mash. Extra reins and bridles hung on nails nearby, and an open box of spurs was on a small stool. A grooming brush rested on top of the stall rail while a horse blanket was draped over its side.

Ben picked up the blanket. "Hey, this belongs to Jet," he said. "Here, see for yourselves." Ben showed them where Jet's name had been embroidered across a label.

"And those buckets, spurs, and brush? They're from our barn, too," Gracie added with a foot stomp. "And that's one of Cookie's bridles, the one I've been looking for. I'd recognize it anywhere. So, this is where the thief has been stashing our ranch's stuff."

"I wonder if these apples are also from your ranch,"

Lexi said as she pointed to a basket of withered fruit.

Ben picked up one to inspect. "Yep," he said, lightly tossing it up and down. "The same variety we grow in our back orchard—and the same kind we pelted the Phantom Rider with during his last raid." He smirked.

His last comment gave the others a much-needed chuckle.

Ben and Lanny turned their attention to the floor of the livery stable. "Are you noticing what I'm noticing?" Ben asked.

Lanny nodded and slowly smiled. "Ah, ha. I do believe I see extra horse tracks," he replied with his best imitation of his British, fictional detective hero, Sherlock Holmes.

"One horse's tracks. And not just any horse. An Arabian's, I'm pretty sure," Ben added. "And one without shoes—since his hard feet are already built for endurance riding."

"Lightning!" all six shouted at once.

CHAPTER SIXTEEN

· ✧ ·

The Phantom Rider's Lair

"I'd say we've just found where the Phantom stables his horse," Lexi replied. She squeezed Rani's forearm until the girl pulled it away. "Sorry, Rani. My bad habit again."

"Here's more proof," Gracie added. She held up what she had just picked out of the grooming brush. "White horsehair."

The kids were so pleased that they shouted "yes" with fist pumps.

Moki said, "So, Lightning must be off with the Phantom Rider during the day and probably returns here sometime in the night. But where does the Phantom go after leaving here—and how does he travel without his horse?"

"Assuming he ever leaves without his horse," Lexi replied.

Lanny's eyebrows raised. "Lexi, that's spooky, but brilliant. If you're right—"

Rani was expertly redoing her thick, windblown braid

and hadn't been tuned in to Lanny and Lexi's conversation. "And where are they now?"

Lanny shrugged, walked over to the livery door, and glanced out. "No rain yet, and we're okay on time. I say we search the rest of this town for more clues—and the Phantom. Even though Lightning is gone, we don't know for sure if the Phantom is."

Everyone's eyes grew large thinking of the heightened possibility of an encounter with the scary marauder. But they were, after all, six detectives on a mission, and each agreed whole-heartedly to Lanny's idea. After quickly stabling and caring for their horses, they dashed outside and closed the livery door as quietly as possible. If the Phantom or anyone else was around, they didn't want to tip them off.

The group made their way across Main Street. Lanny momentarily imagined that they had traveled back in time. He half expected a couple of disgruntled cowboys to come charging out of the saloon up ahead any second for a shoot-out in the middle of the street. The others, very much in the present, were glancing at windows to see if the Phantom was spying on them. As far as they could tell, they were alone.

In addition to the saloon, the row of buildings on the left once housed a barber shop, a dressmaker's shop, the local dry goods store, and a hotel. Across the street were the former sheriff's office, a telegraph office, a post office, and a bank. Farther up the street were the church and its cemetery, and the old schoolhouse. There were no students, teachers, preachers, or anyone else in sight now.

"Let's check out the saloon first," Lanny said. The others joined him as they stepped carefully over broken sections of the raised, wooden sidewalk.

Moki was the first to push open the high swinging saloon doors and step inside. Just as he did, he heard something shuffle, followed by a dreaded buzzing sound.

"Freeze, Moki!" Lanny said, grabbing the boy's arm. He didn't need to signal his friend a second time that a deadly danger was nearby.

Not two feet from Moki's legs and just inside the saloon were two large, surprised sidewinders. They had quickly coiled to ward off the intruders, and if they sprang, their sharp, venomous fangs could easily reach well above his boots.

Moki complied the best he could with Lanny's command, but his normally tanned face had already turned pale. The boy silently chided himself on his carelessness though quickly turned his attention to survival. His goal now was not to pass out and land on top of the rattlers. And he hoped he could successfully contain his trembling.

As the group of kids stood petrified for what seemed to Moki like an eternity, the six-foot-long snakes finally uncoiled and left, zigzagging rapidly across the dusty floor and disappearing behind an ancient player piano against a wall.

Moki started breathing again and passed his sleeve across his forehead to mop up the rivers of perspiration. In a shaking voice, he said, "Uh, let's skip this building. I'm

not in the mood for any piano singalongs today, anyway."
He held his hands over his racing heart. "*I inaina naheka.*"

A puzzled Gracie looked at Lexi, who translated, "I
think he said he hates snakes." The two girls nodded.

Lanny slapped Moki on the back. "It's a deal, bro.
Let's go check out the hotel instead." He moved ahead to
lead the search, hoping it would refocus his pale friend.

Moki turned to Rani. "You were right. This place is
literally crawling with *naheka*." He moved to a safer spot at
the back of the group, making a mental note never to be the
first one to enter a building again that might contain "fangs
of death."

"I didn't intend to be right. Sorry about that, Moki,"
Rani replied sympathetically.

Lexi added, "That goes for me, too, Moki. Teasing you
wasn't nice at all."

"Thanks, but it bears repeating—I love California, but
not its snakes. They're what I call 'trouble in Paradise.'" He
managed to flash a slight smile. Then Moki, still trembling
slightly, and the three girls moved forward to catch up with
Lanny and Ben.

A few yards ahead was the Rainbow Flats Hotel. It was
a large building with a true second story, not a façade like
some of the other structures. Lanny figured the movie studio
that had made a film here a few years ago must have fixed
up the place, since the outside was in better condition than
the rest of the town.

Lexi turned the old crystal knob of the inviting wooden

door with its etched glass panels. Everyone did a quick critter check around the floor before stepping across the hotel's threshold. "Nice and warm in here," Lexi whispered. "Even better, no wind."

"And, so far, no snakes," Moki added. He continued checking all around himself.

The inside was also relatively clean and in good condition. A check-in desk with its empty, pigeon-holed mail slots was to the right, and a T-shaped, polished wooden staircase wound upwards from the center of the plush lobby. The kids were amazed that the beautiful red velvet Victorian furniture left behind in the dining room by the movie studio was still there.

Rani whispered, "If I were the Phantom, this is where I'd choose to hide."

"Good thinking, Rani," Lanny said. "In that case, I think we should stay together even if it takes us more time to investigate."

The others, especially Moki, nodded.

The dining room held no clues, so the group tiptoed to the large hotel kitchen in the back. The kids figured it must have been where the movie crew ate since it contained many newer pots and pans. There were cobwebs, but not as many as the kids had seen draping the other buildings. And no Phantom.

Across the room sat a plain wooden table and two chairs. From nearby, Rani said, "Look at these big footprints all over the floor. They look fresh."

The other kids gathered around the area where Rani stood. Indeed, undisturbed prints, all the same size, were visible.

"Round toe. Square heel," Ben said, then sighed. "But so are most cowboy boots."

With hiked eyebrows and a pointing finger, Rani said, "Check out the table."

There on the table was one place setting. A tin plate contained a bit of buttered bread that was still soft and some browned but moist apple peelings. The chipped cup by the plate held a few leftover swallows of black coffee.

"Cold," Lanny said, setting the cup back down right where he had found it.

A search of the cupboards revealed some canned goods and other nonperishable foods. Their expiration dates showed they had been purchased recently.

"I'm feeling like Goldilocks, except I'm not a blond or a girl," Moki said.

Lexi added, "Well, I am a girl, but a brunette, not a blonde, and I still have no intention of eating the food or sitting in the chair."

She and Moki shared a welcome chuckle.

"But let's at least go upstairs and check out the beds," Lanny replied with a smirk.

"A funny and logical comeback, bro, but still a good idea," Moki said. "You lead the way, Sherlock." He pushed his friend forward.

The six headed back to the hotel lobby, still on tiptoe

as well as on constant lookout for the Phantom. Each knew he could be around any corner. They made it to the staircase safely. Fortunately, the carpeted stairs didn't creak. They climbed upward and moved down the long hallway, trying each door. Keys didn't seem necessary. All the empty rooms were unlocked—except the last one at the end of the hall.

Ben darted back downstairs to the check-in desk and luckily found a skeleton key in a drawer, then rejoined the others. After hearing nothing from pressing his ear against the door, he inserted the key into the lock, turned it, and thrust the door open.

A sight met their eyes. Light from an open curtain revealed that an unmade bed had obviously been slept in recently, given the indentations in the modern sheets and pillowcases. Kerosene lanterns and some matchboxes were on the nightstand and a table. Various articles of a man's clothing littered the floor. No one recognized the items as belonging to anyone in particular. Rani cautiously opened the chest of drawers but found nothing remarkable, just some more old mostly black shirts and socks.

Lexi wandered over to a door. *Probably a closet,* she thought. She pulled on the knob. When it opened, she gasped. Lexi reached up and took the object that had riveted her attention off the closet shelf. "Guys, you better come see this. I think we hit pay dirt."

There could be no doubt as to what it was.

CHAPTER SEVENTEEN

· ✧ ·

Dangerous Barn Talk

"A black ski mask!" Lanny said, taking the knitted object that Lexi handed to him. "I think we found the Phantom Rider's lair and the answer to Moki's two questions, namely, 'Where does the Phantom go after leaving Lightning, and how does he travel without his horse.' The answer to both is . . . he doesn't."

"So the Phantom must spend the night here and ride Lightning during the day, too," Lexi added as she further inspected the mask inside and out.

"Which means Lightning could be his main or only horse," Ben said.

"Or he travels somewhere else during the day and, to keep his identity a secret, changes horses," Moki replied.

Lanny's eyebrows raised as they often did when he heard a good hypothesis.

"And he would probably also need to change clothes," Gracie added.

The others, including Ben, looked at her and nodded.

She continued, "Most of these clothes are dark colored. I bet they aren't what he would normally wear in the daytime. All the better to disguise himself. These items must make up some of his Phantom costume."

Rani gave Gracie two thumbs up and a big smile. The group looked over the clothing but couldn't find any clues to a person's identity. They were careful to return each rumpled item to its original place.

Rani turned to Lexi. "Say, is there any hair inside that mask?" Lanny had returned it to his sister to hold.

"Not that I can see, girlfriend. Just some yucky dandruff. But good thinking."

Moki glanced around and with a shaky voice said, "I say let's get out of here, *wiki-wiki*. No telling when the Phantom might return."

Everyone agreed. Each was certain they had indeed found where the Phantom Rider holed up. And it made total sense to them since Rainbow Flats was apparently where Lexi and Ben had seen him heading at breakneck speed on Lightning the night before.

Lexi returned the ski mask to the shelf exactly as she had found it.

Ben held back. "Wait. Shouldn't we take the mask to show the sheriff and to prevent the Phantom from using it anymore as his disguise?" He reached for it.

Moki was quick to reply. "No, dude. Stop. The mask is evidence the police need to gather legally. If we take it, we could possibly be accused of stealing property that isn't ours and obstructing an investigation."

Gracie stomped her foot. "But not the stuff we found in the barn. It's ours."

"Sorry, Gracie," Moki replied. "Yes, it's yours, but the police need to collect it with search warrants. Again, if we take it, we could be arrested for tampering with evidence and possibly preventing the Phantom's prosecution later."

The girl's shoulders slumped. "I guess you're right, Moki. But I don't like it."

"Whoa, dude, you do know the law," Ben said.

"Can't help it, being the son of a policeman." Moki was proud of his dad but tried not to smile since he knew his information was a disappointment to the Mayfield kids.

"In addition to not taking anything, I suggest we cover up any evidence of our visit here today," Lanny said. "We don't want the Phantom to know we've found his lair."

"Because if he did, he might get spooked in the wrong way and relocate," Lexi added.

The group went downstairs after locking the room's door. Ben returned the skeleton key to the exact spot where he had gotten it from the desk drawer. They checked the kitchen floor, grabbed a broom, and gently swept away their footprints—but not the Phantom's. Lanny peeked outside to ensure the man had not come riding back into town. No Phantom, but a cold drizzle was now falling.

Gracie pulled her poncho closer. "Here comes the rain. We better get home fast."

"But not before we cover more tracks, especially in the livery," Lanny replied.

The kids proceeded quickly to the livery stable and got their horses. After they led their mounts outside, Ben and Gracie held all the reins as the detectives gathered some shrubbery to use as track erasers. Lexi and Rani cleaned up inside the stables while Moki and Lanny took care of the outside. They followed on foot and swept behind the horses until Lanny was sure they had done enough. Then, the kids tossed the shrubbery pieces as far as they could. He was glad the rain and wind would also help wipe out evidence of their visit.

"*Aloha,* Rainbow Flats and fangs of death," Moki said as he turned Grandma toward home, joining his friends. "*Mahalo* for the info, but I'm glad you're now in my rearview mirror."

Within minutes, the riders had put a good distance between themselves and the ghost town. The mournful church steeple bell had tolled its farewell but was at last receding. Their attention now turned to the intensifying storm. A steady downpour and brisk winds made the kids thankful they had worn good waterproof gear and warm clothing.

Lanny scanned the terrain as they rode on but saw no sign of the Phantom Rider. As much as he wanted to discover the man's identity, he did not want an encounter with the marauder so far from home. His peace of mind was offset, however, by a disappointing confirmation as the riders crossed back onto the Gold Mine Acres Ranch property: Glancing up at the rain-lashed northern mountains, he knew they would definitely not be exploring today where he so desperately wanted to go.

Soon, they arrived at the ranch.

Even though it was only just past three o'clock, the storm's darkness meant the lights were on inside the bunkhouse's common area. It looked inviting as the weary riders approached. The group quickly but efficiently put up their horses in the barn and dashed to the welcoming bunkhouse. As they entered, they noticed Catherine and Lionel were holed up inside with Mrs. Mayfield, Uncle Rocky, Jax, and Rufus.

"Hey, welcome home, travelers," Mrs. Mayfield said as she glanced up from the table. "Go take off your wet gear and join us."

"Yeah, then come see what we're doing," Catherine said. "Uncle Rocky's taught us how to play Texas hold 'em. It's a fun kind of poker. Mrs. Mayfield already knew how to play. She said even though betting is legal in California, we can't yet. We have to be at least eighteen years old first."

"Yeah, and I'm winning and having fun—even without betting," Lionel replied. He grinned as he pointed to his column of tally marks on the sheet next to Uncle Rocky.

"These two kids caught on fast," Uncle Rocky said. "Aunt Maisie's foot is better, so she kicked me out of the kitchen today. Mr. Mayfield is helping her, but I'll check on them later."

Lionel looked up from his cards. "The rain made us come indoors. No more riding today. I think the horses were glad. We've really been workin' 'em."

Catherine added, "Before that, Jax and Rufus taught us how to saddle and unsaddle our horses."

"Bathing and brushing the horses was fun, too, but not mucking out the stable." Lionel said, pinching his nostrils. "But as Jax says, 'Most everything that's worth anything has a price. So, stop bellyachin', and just do it.'"

Jax nodded, pleased that Lionel was applying the expression to real life.

All six kids congratulated Catherine and Lionel on having a great day.

Uncle Rocky invited the kids to join the card game. Lexi, Rani, and Moki immediately pulled up chairs despite still being somewhat damp from their adventure. Gracie thanked the man but said she wanted to go catch up on her sticker book collection. With permission from her mother, she left for the ranch house.

Then, Lanny and Ben took Mrs. Mayfield aside a few steps. They shared with her that they were sure they had found the Phantom Rider's and Lightning's lairs. They included all the important details about the Mayfields' stolen property in the barn and the black ski mask in the hotel.

"You kids did a great job today, and good thinking on not taking anything. Thanks for letting me know. I'm going to go call the sheriff's office right now. He was supposed to come over this afternoon and play chess with the kids but couldn't at the last minute. The deputy called today to say there were no leads yet on those lights on the mountain or our recent ranch thefts. He couldn't get up on the ridge due to the storm." She left for the ranch house to make the call and to update her husband on the kids' discoveries.

The two boys quickly joined the card game, but Lanny had trouble concentrating. His mind was on all the work they had to do tomorrow if they were going to solve their case on time.

Meanwhile, Gracie had gotten her box of stickers and thick album from her room with the intention of taking them to her favorite quiet place—the hayloft in the barn. The group's visit to Rainbow Flats had reminded her that she had purchased many sheets of rainbow stickers at Cody's general store a month ago that needed pasting in.

A few minutes later, Gracie entered the barn. It was growing dark and wonderfully quiet except for an occasional rustling sound as a horse moved in its stall. The humid smell of the barn on rainy days gave her a sense of peace. She climbed the old wooden ladder to the hayloft and hunkered down in a thick pile of crunchy straw near the big window to make use of the dwindling light. Lying on her stomach, she lost track of time as she worked away placing various stickers on theme pages. She enjoyed hearing Cookie and the other horses as they softly ate and snorted. She could just spy them through the slats in the loft's floor.

Soon, however, Gracie discovered that she and the horses were not alone. A man's familiar voice drifted upwards, interrupting her reverie. He was on the barn's wall phone below, and his tone sounded frantic.

"Tell the man that today the kids were in Rainbow Flats. . . . Yeah, they found his hideout and where he stables the horse," said the voice. "Uh, huh. That's right. Better let him know, pronto. Tell him I'll meet him there tonight for the paper. It isn't safe for him to keep it anymore. And I hope all of us can wrap up our work on the mountain and clear out soon."

Gracie froze and listened carefully, hoping to hear some names mentioned. But none were. Just "the man." She felt the hair stand up on the back of her neck and must have moved slightly. The person on the phone noticed a few pieces of straw float down from the loft and immediately hung up.

"Okay. Who's up there? I know you're there," said the voice. "Better come on down. Don't make me come up after you."

Gracie was terrified but quickly overcame her fear and used her head. She knew she needed time, so she jumped up and pushed the ladder away from the loft. It clattered to the floor below. Her action would buy her only a few extra seconds, but she intended to make good use of that precious time.

She tried to scream, but her throat was paralyzed as in a nightmare. It was too far down to jump out the window without seriously injuring herself. The girl broke out in a cold sweat, but an idea hit her. With jittery hands, she worked feverishly to leave behind a solid clue.

Next came a bang as the top legs of the ladder hit the loft's edge. The person was coming up after her! She was still trying to finish her task as the climber's irate face crested the floor of the loft.

CHAPTER EIGHTEEN

· ✧ ·

Gracie Mayfield, Deputy Detective

At five o'clock, Gracie didn't show up at the dinner table. Ben hadn't thought anything of her not washing up with the rest of them in the bunkhouse since she was off with her sticker album.

"Well, we know where she is—in her not-so-secret place, the hayloft," Ben said.

His mom agreed. "She does lose track of time when she's working on that album up there. Please go get her, Ben. We'll wait for the two of you for a few minutes before starting dinner."

Ben left but soon returned with a worried expression and something in his hands. "Gracie wasn't there, but look what I found in the hayloft." He held out his sister's sticker album.

On its cover was a name spelled out with Gracie's new rainbow stickers—R-U-F-U-S. The "s" wasn't complete but still obvious. And so was the message.

Mr. and Mrs. Mayfield looked at each other. They knew Gracie's clue signaled that their daughter was in some kind of danger. A million questions swam in their heads, but they tried not to frighten the other kids.

The detectives also sensed something was very wrong.

"Good job, Gracie," Rani said into the air. "What a great clue."

Chairs were quickly pushed back as everyone started to run to the barn. Mrs. Mayfield stopped Catherine and Lionel and told them to stay in the house with Aunt Maisie and Uncle Rocky. The two kids groaned as she ran to join the group.

Mr. Mayfield found Jax relaxing in his quarters—but no Rufus next door in his.

Jax could tell something was amiss and jumped to his feet. "I don't know where he is. We usually eat dinner together but not till later in the evening."

Mr. Mayfield quickly filled him in, and he joined in the investigation. It was Jax who noticed Rufus's old truck was missing.

Mrs. Mayfield had rushed to the barn with the kids. They discovered uneven piles of hay—evidence of a struggle—in the hayloft. She sprinted to the same wall phone Rufus had used and called the sheriff's office for the second time that afternoon. No one picked up, but she left a detailed message on the answering machine and asked the officers to please join them as soon as possible in Rainbow Flats.

In no time, Gracie's parents, Jax, and the five kids were in the van heading for the ghost town. Mr. Mayfield applied as much speed as he safely could on the slick, muddy road that led northeast from the ranch. Moki never dreamed he would be back in that desolate place again, let alone tonight.

No one spoke as the car sped along. A few rays of sunlight glimmered through the leftover pink and gray rainclouds, but the brightness wouldn't last much longer.

When the van finally pulled into the ghost town, the pitch black night had descended. Mr. Mayfield turned off his headlights so as not to announce their arrival. Then, he drove quietly right down the middle of Main Street.

"Look for some lights in a building," his wife said as she scanned both sides of the street.

Soon, Lexi called out, "I see some flickering lights in the old church up ahead."

Mr. Mayfield drove there as quickly but silently as possible so as not to alert anyone inside. He parked nearby, and each person got out of the van without a sound. They had trouble containing their anxiety but tiptoed to the front. Within seconds, Mr. Mayfield yanked open the church door.

"Mom, Dad!" a relieved Gracie yelled. She wasn't tied up and jumped up and dashed out of the church pew toward her parents. Rufus, who had been sitting near her, scrambled to his feet and looked shocked to see the group. Clearly, he was expecting someone else.

Mrs. Mayfield wrapped her daughter in her arms and

kissed the top of her head. "Are you all right, punkin? Did he hurt you?" Mrs. Mayfield wanted to confront Rufus, but she felt that the best way to help her daughter right this moment was to stay calm and focus on her.

Gracie said she was fine now. "He brought me here because I heard what he said on the barn phone. He kept apologizing for having to take me, but he said he had to. He tied me up at first when we got here, so he could go somewhere. But then, he came back and untied me."

Rufus was looking around for a clue as to what he should do. He decided to run. But Jax caught him by the arm and held on tightly before he got far.

"Why, you lowdown, good-for-nothing ingrate," Jax said, shaking the younger man uncontrollably. "After all these years working together. How could you do this to the Mayfields who have been so good to you?"

Mr. Mayfield intervened. "Jax, I, too, have lots of questions." He shot angry looks at Rufus, but stayed near his daughter. "We'll get to the bottom of this once the police take charge. It's best for no one to say or do too much right now. That includes you, Gracie, darlin'. We'll hear your story later as well. For now, I'm glad you're all right."

Jax relaxed his grip on Rufus's arm, made him sit down, and stood guard. All Rufus could do was to stare at the ground and repeatedly say he was sorry for what he had done.

Lexi and Rani were complimenting Gracie on the great clue she had left in the barn when they heard the sound of a car. Lanny went to the door. "The police are here."

Ned Buchanan entered the church and looked surprised to see his work of capturing a kidnapper already accomplished. "Sorry for the delay. Sheriff Buckley is attending to a storm-related issue. What's going on here?"

The deputy began taking statements, first from Gracie. Her parents shook their heads when they heard her tell what Rufus had said on the phone.

Rufus glanced up at the Mayfield parents. "I'm sorry about taking Gracie, really I am. But I had to. What she said is true. I heard what the kids discovered in Rainbow Flats while eavesdropping on Mrs. Mayfield, Ben, and Lanny during the bunkhouse card game. I had to report it."

Everything Rufus said was already obvious but hardly a satisfactory explanation by Mrs. Mayfield's thinking. She told the deputy, "Well, thank goodness for Gracie's clue that led us here to Rainbow Flats."

Soon, the lawman read Rufus the charges against him and his rights and correctly cautioned him to say nothing more until a lawyer could be present back at the sheriff's office. He handcuffed the man and led him to the door. The others watched the deputy put Rufus in the back of the car. Its door had barely closed when Sheriff Buckley pulled up and was filled in on the details.

"Take him to jail, Ned," ordered Sheriff Buckley. "I'll take over here and meet you back in Cody at the office later." The deputy drove away with his prisoner.

"I got your phone messages, Edie," Sheriff Buckley

said. "The one about Gracie and the one earlier about the mountain trespassers. First things first. I've brought a search warrant for the town buildings. Let's go see what you kids found—if you're up for it."

"Are we ever," Gracie said, speaking for the others as she bolted for the church door.

Rani watched the girl gallop off and chuckled. "I'd say Gracie's earned the title 'Deputy Detective.'"

"I'll second that title—and a fearless one at that," Lexi replied.

Gracie's parents stared after their amazing daughter, who gave no sign of having been in danger.

CHAPTER NINETEEN

· ✧ ·

Papa Mayfield's Claim

Gracie was happy to be safely reunited with her family after the incident with Rufus. She led the sheriff and the entire group across the street from the Rainbow Flats' church to the hotel.

The other kids quickly took up the nickname "Deputy Detective Gracie" and praised the girl for her bravery. She had never smiled so hard in her life.

Once inside the hotel, the sheriff snapped on his large, powerful flashlight and handed a battery-operated lantern to Gracie.

"Careful!" Moki called out. "There are rattlers everywhere in this town."

"My boy," the sheriff said, placing a strong hand on Moki's shoulder. "If it ever comes down to a rattler or me, I'd feel sorry for the rattler."

Ben snatched the skeleton key from the desk drawer. Then, they all trooped upstairs to the Phantom Rider's lair, unlocked the door, and entered. Lexi ran to the closet door and flung it open. To her dismay, the black ski mask was gone!

Her shoulders slumped. "It was right here." The kids backed her up, saying they, too, had seen it.

"Well, I'm for searching this room some more," Lanny said. "We did leave in a hurry this afternoon because of the storm."

Gracie set her lantern down on a bureau to light the room to everyone's advantage. To assist further, Mrs. Mayfield lit one of the room's kerosene lanterns. Then, everyone fanned out and started looking in drawers and under the bed. Still no mask.

But within minutes, Moki had found something. "Look, you guys. There are some loose floorboards over here, a little ways under the bed."

The sheriff went out to his car and soon returned with a hammer and chisel. In a short time, four squeaky floorboard pieces were raised. Their efforts paid off. Inside was an unlocked black metal box about one foot square.

"Here, Gracie, Deputy Detective," the sheriff said as he handed it to the girl. "Won't you do the honors of opening it for us?" All the kids including Ben added their encouragement.

Gracie was thrilled to be given the task. She pulled on the lid's small top handle. The box popped open effortlessly.

All eyes stared inside. There they saw—not a ski mask—but a faded and soiled manila envelope. The words

"Cody Assay Office" were still legible in embossed, faded black ink from an ancient printing press. The girl peeked inside to find something made of parchment paper. It was a document of some kind. The sheriff carefully pulled it out with a gloved hand.

Everyone seemed to hold their breath.

"'Deed of Claim . . .'" the sheriff read out loud. "It's Papa Mayfield's gold mine claim!"

Everyone gasped. After all these years, they'd finally found it.

The sheriff held up the document, which showed Papa's claim had been duly registered in Cody by the deputy marshal turned miner on July 9, 1876. And most important, it contained the coordinates to Papa's mine.

"Woohoo!" Lanny shouted with a fist pump. "This will help us tomorrow for sure."

"Moki, great job finding it," Mrs. Mayfield said.

"*Mahalo*. All in the line of duty." Moki nevertheless beamed ear to ear.

"And you, too, Lanny, for insisting we keep searching," Mr. Mayfield added.

"I hope it will make our work tomorrow that much easier," the boy replied.

It was Ben's turn. "And you guys have helped give back to my family and me not only my sister, but also an important piece of our history." He sincerely hugged Gracie as their two proud parents looked on, nodding.

Soon, however, congratulations changed to big

questions and a revelation. Where, when, and how did the Phantom get the claim? Why did he have it? Who, if anyone, had given it to him?

Lanny said, "I think it's fair to say that if he had this claim with its mine coordinates, he's probably already used it." There was no question in his mind that tomorrow's search on the north rim of the mountain was absolutely critical. He also knew that the search might bring them face to face with the Phantom.

The group continued examining the room for a few more minutes. Neither the sheriff nor the Mayfield parents recognized any of the well-worn clothing as belonging to anyone they knew.

"Maybe we're dealing with an unknown Phantom Rider, or 'The Man,' as Gracie heard Rufus refer to him," Lexi said. "A stranger. Someone not from around Cody."

Rani replied, "You might be right, bestie girlfriend. And Lightning seems to be a mystery to everyone, too."

"If true, solving our case could be much more complicated," Moki said.

Lanny grimaced.

The group pondered these ideas as they left the hotel to continue their search in the livery. Once inside the stables, Ben pointed to the blanket and to the grooming brush with white hair. To the boy's surprise, it also held a few leftover strands from Jet's golden coat. "Look, sheriff. This hair belongs to my horse."

"And here are the buckets, Cookie's bridle, and a

saddle club kid's suitcase," Gracie said to her interested parents and the amazed sheriff. Some items had the name "Mayfield" on them.

Sheriff Buckley proceeded to bag up the items to take for fingerprinting. Then, he turned and handed Lanny a pair of police gloves to put on before giving him the claim envelope. "Get any information right now from the deed of claim that you think you'll need for tomorrow's search. I have to take it with me as evidence and for fingerprinting."

Lanny handled the document around its edges so as not to disrupt any possible fingerprints, noting what he thought the detectives would need, including the mine's coordinates. Lexi saw her brother's crafty smile and knew he had just gotten a critical piece of information. She also knew better than to ask him about it right that moment. He would reveal his findings in good time.

Then, the group headed back to the church for their cars to go home. Sheriff Buckley had said that he would continue searching the rest of the town by daylight as soon as he could. He also promised to try to join the kids on the mountain ridge the next day and cautioned them to be careful. "Your cell phones won't work well up there, so you won't be able to call me. But I'll plan to meet you there as early as I can."

It had been an eventful and, ultimately, productive day. And if the detectives were going to solve their case on time, tomorrow would need to be even busier.

CHAPTER TWENTY

· ✧ ·

More Key Discoveries

By the morning after Rufus's arrest, word had already spread in Cody and to neighboring ranches that the Mayfields were now in need of a new hired hand. The Youth Saddle Club required at least two arena workers to run smoothly, so it was important for the Mayfields and Jax to take care of this new business immediately. Fortunately, the ranch's house phone had started ringing nonstop at seven in the morning with eager applicants. As a result, though, the morning schedule and activities had to be altered to accommodate interviews. Ben and Gracie's mother had an idea.

"Yes, Edie, I think you've come up with a great solution," Aunt Maisie told her. "Uncle Rocky and I would be happy to have Cat and Lion's help in the kitchen today. Right?"

"You know it, Aunt Maisie," Uncle Rocky replied. "No more crutches, but you still need to be careful, so we can dance up a storm at tomorrow night's party. We do have lots of food to prepare today for the shindig. Two extra pairs of hands and feet will be welcome."

"Yay!" Catherine and Lionel screamed. They were sorry to have to miss riding horses for the day. But baking a mountain of party cookies and a big sheet cake for the celebration would be more fun, especially if they got to lick the bowls. The two quickly began pulling measuring cups and mixing bowls from the cupboards.

Mrs. Mayfield laughed. "Well, I'm glad all of you are being such good sports. I wouldn't think of leaving the kids indoors if there had been only one adult in the kitchen. But Uncle Rocky, once again, you've saved the day. You, too, as always, Aunt Maisie."

Uncle Rocky replied, "These are two great kids. It just goes to show you that putting kids in the right environment, like here at your ranch, can make all the difference in the world."

Breakfast was eaten and cleared away quickly. This worked equally well for the six other kids, who were already saddling their horses and anxious to be off to look for Papa's gold mine. Fortunately, the weather was cooperating. Sunshine and blue skies had replaced rain and wind. The Mayfields said it was safe as far as the weather for the kids to head to the high mountains. Lanny packed the skeleton key, photo, his notes from the claim, and Rani's dad's notes in his knapsack, along with his gold test kit.

Lexi was adjusting Toby's cinch but glanced up and

said, "So Lanny, give. I saw that look on your face last night. What did you learn from the claim that might help our search today?"

Lanny was holding Sam's reins. He smiled and replied, "Just that the mine is definitely on that high northern mountain ridge. It described the mine's location as facing mostly north."

"That's exactly where Lexi and I saw the bright lights," Ben exclaimed, dropping Jet's new grooming brush.

Gracie stroked Cookie's mane. "And don't forget what I heard Rufus tell the person on the phone—that they needed to 'wrap up their work on the mountain' soon."

Moki, who was bent over cleaning Grandma's hooves, stopped, looked up at the group, and said, "It's still sounding to me as if the Phantom Rider and company have definitely beaten us to the gold mine, given those weird lights up there and what Gracie overheard."

"If so, then it's up to all of us to reclaim it for the Mayfields," Rani replied, raising Ginger's stirrups to accommodate her own height.

At that moment, Mr. and Mrs. Mayfield came into the barn to see the kids off. Ben's dad held Jet steady while the boy mounted. "Now, Ben," he said loudly enough for all the kids to hear. "Your mother and I are still nervous about what happened to Gracie. So, let's be clear. You and the others are not to take any unnecessary chances. Your explorations today are to be just a fact-finding mission, a stakeout at best. You kids are not to confront anyone. And keep your eyes on

Gracie. If your mom and I didn't have to meet with hired hand candidates today, you know we'd be going with you. Do you understand?"

"Yes, sir. I promise to tell you every detail when we get back," Ben said.

"You better," his dad said. "The sheriff is supposed to show up to help you kids this morning. Or maybe the deputy—I don't know. They weren't very chit-chatty about the details. Just watch for one of them. I'm still a bit worried, though, about . . ."

Mrs. Mayfield lightly tugged on her husband's hand. "Let them go, Ezra. They've got this." On second thought, she spoke up, so all the riders could hear. "Just be careful, all of you. About entering the mine, of course, but also because of the lights Ben and Lexi saw in that area. If you feel in danger, we expect all of you to hightail it out of there immediately. We'll be watching for you."

"And if we don't return . . ." Ben teased.

His mother interrupted him. "Not funny, Benjamin. If you don't return by three o'clock, we'll personally come looking for you. You can count on it."

Just then, Mrs. Mayfield's cell phone rang, and she stepped away to answer it. The kids made their final preparations and were ready to leave when she returned to share the sheriff's update.

"Rufus isn't talking," she said. "He's refusing to say who 'The Man' is, what business is being conducted, and who else might be involved. At least they now know the paper

Gracie heard Rufus mention was the gold mine claim."

Lanny smiled to himself, imagining the look on the Phantom's face when he returned to his lair and discovered the pried-up floorboards, the missing claim, and no livery supplies. But the boy was annoyed and worried that the black ski mask was apparently still in the Phantom's possession. And they hadn't found any other distinctive pieces from his black riding outfit at the hotel, at least not according to Ben.

Relishing what they had already accomplished in their case, the six kids now rode with their heads held high for the northwestern mountainous rim of the Mayfield ranch as fast as safety would allow. Ben and Gracie were in the lead. They had to ride more slowly at times than Lanny wanted due to some slippery spots from yesterday's rain. But they made good progress nonetheless.

"Okay, everybody," Lanny called. "Be on the lookout for granite and schist intersecting."

Lexi replied, "Also, Rani's dad said to look for gold-bearing, dirty reddish-brown quartz."

"Don't forget ore-car tracks," Moki said. "But, hopefully, no snake tracks."

"And look for those twin pine trees from Papa's old photo," Rani reminded them.

Ben added, "Of course, there might still be a door on the mine entrance. We couldn't tell from the photo. Remember? And loose rocks or small boulders at the entrance would be good markers as well."

"I hope we can find out what caused those weird lights Ben and Lexi saw during the campout," Gracie said. Cookie bobbed her head and snorted her agreement.

"I feel today will be our lucky day," Rani shouted, followed by a "Yee-haw!"

Lanny and the others joined in and waved their hats, too. Everyone rode on in high spirits, especially Gracie, who now felt like a fully accepted member of the group—even by her brother.

The warm morning passed uneventfully. As the group continued higher into the mountains, an occasional rabbit would skitter out of a bush, or a scurrying lizard stop abruptly on a sunny rock. Melodious birdsong gave the false impression that the kids were just out for a casual ride. In reality, each was getting more nervous about what they would find once they reached their destination. The long-lost gold mine? No gold mine? Trespassers? Maybe even the Phantom Rider himself? Hopefully, the sheriff or deputy.

To calm her jitters, Lexi asked if anyone remembered what they had learned from the lessons their tutor Bruce had shared with them about gold mining in 1850s California.

Rani was first to reply. "That gold was worth about twenty cents an ounce back in olden times, which was good money."

"Yeah," Moki added, "But the cost of living in the mining camps was expensive. Miners had to pay a lot for their food and supplies that often had to be shipped from far away."

Lanny said, "Just so happens, this morning, I Googled to see what an ounce of gold is worth now. Any guesses?"

"Oh, maybe . . . five hundred dollars an ounce." Ben offered. The others shared their guesses.

"Would you believe more like 1,785 dollars—plus the dealer's premium," Lanny replied.

Moki's eyebrows practically hit his hairline as he sucked in his breath. "Wow! A few chunks of gold could buy me my own private island paradise."

"Where you could park your pirate ship!" Gracie said with a smile.

Moki winked at her. "True, but I believe the word is *moor,* not park. Arrgh!"

"Stop, everybody," Rani said as she brought Ginger to a sudden halt. Her tone was serious, and her words came rapidly. "Look. I'm seeing streaks of granite and schist in the hillside. And dirty quartz." She smiled, pointing to the rock face on their left.

Lanny was almost breathless. "You're right, Rani. Let's watch for other signs. We might be close to finding Papa's mine. In fact, we should be, according to the claim."

"Yes, we're approaching the right area," Ben confirmed. "This is the northwestern rim."

Lexi jumped off Toby and pointed to the ground ahead. "Look, guys. Boulders and rock piles. But I don't see any mine entrance. Also, no ore-car tracks. Just a huge thicket of brush."

Moki had already ridden to the area just beyond where

Lexi stood. "And no Phantom." *Thank goodness*, he thought. "But I wonder where the sheriff or deputy is."

The air was laden with pollen, which caused Grandma to snort loudly and repeatedly. Without warning, a rush of wind blew past them. The horse reared, throwing Moki hard against the hillside. Lexi ran forward and wisely grabbed Grandma's reins to keep her from bolting off the nearby precipice. Moki was too surprised to speak.

Suddenly, bats swarmed around them! Dozens of screeching, unhappy bats of all sizes were escaping chaotically in a rush of black streaks and leathery wings from somewhere behind and above the boy, who now lay sprawled in the brush.

But Moki found his voice. "Aww!" he shouted as he flung his arms wildly to avoid being engulfed by the winged creatures rousted from their dark haven. "First snakes, now bats. Why me? I'm not the park ranger. More *pilikia*."

"No, Moki, but you are an angel," Lexi said as the others ran to help. "A gold-plated angel. You call this trouble? Do you know where you've landed with sweet Grandma's help?"

"Not in a snake pit, I hope," he replied as he stood quickly, dusting himself off, and looking around for any crawling critters.

"No snake pit, Moki. You and the bats have exposed the opening of a cave!" Rani said. "This brush is probably just a blind. It could have been purposely placed here to cover the opening. I wonder . . ."

Everyone, including Moki, started pulling the thorny brambles away. In no time, they uncovered a large cave entrance. A few sleepy bats that had stayed behind were heard squeaking inside. But what was more amazing was what the kids found surrounding the cave. The large, rectangular opening's perimeter was bordered on its top and sides by wooden beams. And two rotted wooden door halves had been discarded and lay in a heap to the left behind more brush.

Lanny quickly pulled away the debris. "Ben, Gracie, I think we've found Papa's long-lost gold mine! But before we get too excited, let's make some tests first." He grabbed the skeleton key and the photo from his knapsack as everyone gathered around him.

"Thank goodness no one else is around here right now. And no snakes," Moki said.

"Guys, look. There are the pine trees." Rani pointed up. Indeed, above the cave were the two trees, now ancient, but looking down on them as if they were Papa's personal signposts.

"Woohoo, a monument marker sign, too." Ben had found a disintegrated post with a sign not far from the opening. From the notes he'd taken last night, Lanny confirmed that the sign's claim number matched the number on Papa's claim.

"For fun, let's try the key in the mine door to see if that's what it was used for," Lexi said. She clasped her hands behind herself just in time to stop from squeezing her brother's forearm.

Lanny turned to pass Lexi the key. "Not me," she said. "I think that honor should go to Ben and Gracie." The other three detectives agreed.

Ben took the key from Lanny's outstretched arm. His hand was shaking as he approached the old door and inserted the big key into the rusty mechanism. Gracie sat next to him with her hands wrapped around his, helping him turn it. It refused their efforts.

Undaunted, they pressed harder. Then, with a resounding click, it worked.

"Yay!" everyone yelled as they danced around the entrance in celebration. Even the horses seemed to join in as they skittered in place.

"My parents will go crazy happy when we tell them we found Papa's mine," Ben said. He grabbed his sister and hugged her. "Thanks so much, you guys—and you too, Gracie."

Gracie knew she had never been as completely accepted by Ben as she was right this moment. Being a detective was harder work than she had imagined, but it had been worth every second. She now felt the same was true for being Ben's little sister.

Lexi, Moki, and Lanny said it was definitely an extended team effort.

Meanwhile, Rani, always curious, had already wandered around a bend to the right of the mine.

"Guys!" she called out, startling everyone. "You better come look at what I found around the corner."

CHAPTER TWENTY-ONE

· ✧ ·

Hilltop Construction

The kids stared at Rani's discovery—a long, windowless shed hugging the hillside just beyond the mine. It wasn't what they had expected at all. From the building's appearance, it had been constructed recently and hurriedly. Clearly, someone had known where the mine was this whole time, but they'd kept that information to themselves.

Beyond the shed was a steep dirt trail that led from the mountain and wound down onto the desert floor far below. Lexi snapped her fingers. "Ben, this is the path the Phantom Rider and Lightning must have taken when you and I saw them heading for Rainbow Flats by moonlight Wednesday night."

"I think this proves he's in this gold mine caper," Lanny said, "whatever and whoever else it involves, right up to his black ski mask."

Lexi rolled her eyes at her brother. "I never doubted it, but I know. Evidence."

"Lanny, I think you're right," Ben replied. He pointed at the ground around them. "Lots of small horse tracks here."

"But how exactly are Rainbow Flats, the Phantom Rider, and this camp tied together?" Rani asked with a frown. "That's what we need to figure out."

Lanny was inspecting the building's door. "First, let's see what this shed's used for. . . . Darn. As I suspected, it's locked." He grunted as he tugged on the combination lock.

"Not a problem," Rani called out to their left. "There are some big, loose boards around this side of the building." She started tugging on one. "Yes! We can squeeze in through here."

Rani and Lanny started pulling on four of the boards. Two came free. The other two swiveled to either side, held only by a single nail at the top. Without a word or any bit of hesitation, Rani pushed herself through the opening. Within seconds, Lanny heard a muffled, "Whoa!" from her. He quickly joined her inside.

"That 'whoa' wasn't because you discovered a snake pit in there, was it?" Moki called out.

"No, bro," Lanny replied in a muffled tone, "but come see what we've found."

Moki's hesitation was all Lexi, Ben, and Gracie needed. They rushed past him, and soon, they were on their bellies crawling inside.

"Looks like a dirty business to me," Moki said into the opening, "but here goes." Being the most muscular of the group, he had a tight squeeze even getting into the opening. "Uh, can someone please give me a hand?" Next, he heard a round of applause and some chuckles coming from his friends. "Ha, ha, ha. Very funny, you guys. Now, really. Would someone pull on me?"

"Sure thing, bro," Lanny said, grabbing Moki's outstretched arms. Soon, Moki was inside the sooty building. Sunshine trickled in through gaps in the wall boards and from the opening they had made. All six started laughing at one another, claiming each was grimier than the other.

Gracie said, "Well, Moki, now you *are* dirty enough to be a pirate."

Lexi reached over and made an S-shaped squiggle on Moki's dusty cheek. "There. That's the only snake in here. Arrgh!" She and Gracie laughed even more.

Moki quickly rubbed it off. "*Ole he kūo'o*—uh, I mean, not funny."

Rani's attention was on their surroundings. "Lights!" she exclaimed. She'd found at least half a dozen poles, lights, and long wires. In addition, there was other mining equipment such as shovels, pickaxes, wheelbarrows, a generator, and battered metal buckets. There were also a couple of black lights, the kind sometimes used by miners to make minerals glow in the dark.

"Seems to me there's only one explanation," Lanny said. "These fixtures get set up so the Phantom and his friends can illegally mine and steal gold from the Mayfields' property by night. Then, the thieves stash the equipment in the shed by day for safe-keeping until they return for their next looting operation."

Ben replied with a frown, "Yeah, and that could explain the strange lights Lexi and I saw while we were camping out the other night."

Gracie added, "And it could explain what Rufus meant about working on the mountain."

"That's right," Rani said. "Good remembering, Gracie. But where is the gold they've already mined?"

"Good question, Rani," Lanny replied. "We need to find out, and fast. From the looks of the tools, I'd say they've been used a lot. Probably for months. I have no doubt the miners have been successful so far. And they probably intend to keep mining and stealing."

"But not for much longer," Moki said as he, Lanny, and Ben did a three-way high five.

Lanny said, "Okay, let's get out of here and reattach the boards we removed. Hopefully, no one will know we've been inside. We have to leave these other things here until the sheriff arrives."

Moki nodded in agreement. No one argued this time.

With that, the kids exited as they had entered with Moki again needing an assist. Then, they hammered the boards back in place with a rock and stood admiring their work.

Lexi said, "We did a great job. I'd never guess anyone had messed with them."

"Let's hope you're right, girlfriend," Rani replied as the two hugged.

Then, the group started back toward the mine entrance where they had tied up their horses.

"As for the gold ore, I doubt they carried it out of here after each visit," Lanny said. "I bet at least some of it's still around here somewhere."

"Well, it's definitely not in the shed. Let's check at the mine," Rani suggested.

"But we can't go inside," Moki reminded them as they walked back toward their first important discovery. "We promised. Besides, I want no part of a bat cave and snake den. I just know there are snakes in there."

Ben replied, "Unfortunately, Moki's right. My parents would have all our heads if we went in there. And I've been in enough trouble lately. But let's keep searching near it." Ben couldn't resist taking a quick glance inside the large opening. He smiled, knowing he was walking on the very ground where his amazing Papa had worked happily so long ago.

Everyone fanned out and started looking for a likely storage place. No one, not even Moki, noticed it was approaching midafternoon, and they had missed lunch. Athletic Rani was already climbing above the mine with Lexi and Gracie not too far behind. The boys concentrated their efforts below while the horses lazily grazed on some brush.

Rani was tired and hot, but she was determined to crest the hill above the mine. Hand over hand she went, careful to watch for rodents and reptiles. Within five minutes, she had reached her goal. That's when she noticed something unusual. There was a hole in a rock slab about a yard square in what was likely the roof of the mine. New-looking steel cables extended from the opening and traveled upward, dodging pine trees to yet another hill. When she looked down into the mine shaft, she saw large, wooden buckets attached to the cables every few feet.

"Guys, get up here, pronto," she called to the others.

Everyone scrambled to join her.

"Wow. A funicular," Lanny said with a grin when he saw the device. "Ingenious."

"A fun—what?" Moki asked.

Lexi groaned, knowing Moki had triggered a definition from Lanny the Lexicon. Moki, realizing what he had done, grimaced and slapped his forehead.

"A *funicular* is a cable railway or inclined elevator for transporting things up or down a hill—in this case, gold ore out of the mine to some place above here, I'll bet. The buckets are the cars. The reinforced-steel cables are the pulleys." Lanny turned to Ben and Gracie. "In addition to all your ancestor's many talents, he was apparently also an engineer. The first funiculars were built in Europe in 1868, so Papa Mayfield must have known about them."

"Whoa, bro," Moki said. "You're beginning to sound like Bruce, the walking computer, who instantly retrieves golden nuggets of knowledge from his brainy hard drive."

Rani said, "The funicular explains why we didn't find any ore-car tracks below."

Gracie planted her hands squarely on her hips and, with a stomp of her foot, replied, "Well, one thing I know. Papa never meant for thieves to use his invention."

"I'm sure you're right," Lexi said. "So now, let's see where this funicular leads."

All six began climbing with renewed energy, using the cables to guide them. Each realized one or more of the gold looters could be nearby, so they continued in silence. The pine tree boughs provided a great shield for the device and for them. Despite having to navigate the foliage, the group made good time. Within ten minutes, they were standing next to a log cabin, similar in craftsmanship and materials to the Gold Mine Acres ranch house.

"Whoa. This has to be Papa's secret mining cabin," Ben said in a hushed tone. "I heard stories about it. Supposedly, he would stay here when it got too late to return to the ranch."

"But we never knew where it was." Gracie beamed. "Until today."

"And he must have stored his gold ore here," Lexi said. "That's why he built the funicular. . . . See? The cables and buckets end right alongside the cabin."

"Well, come on," Rani whispered. "Let's check it out."

The kids were excited but nervous as they sneaked up and quietly circled the cabin. Upon first inspection, it seemed windowless. But Lanny found a large, double-hung window with unbroken glass on the rear wall. A dingy curtain obscured his view of the inside.

Meanwhile, Ben had his ear against the front door. Presently, he said to Moki, "I don't hear anything inside."

"The place is locked up like a fortress," said Moki, pointing to a large, new padlock and hardware that straddled the door and its frame. "Well, someone couldn't have locked himself inside from the outside, right?"

Ben nodded.

Lanny had returned from the back of the cabin and heard Moki's comment. No longer whispering, he said, "I'd say you're right about that, bro. But maybe someone has something else to hide in there. Let's check it out. I found one window. Since no one's home, let's see if we can jiggle the casement and get inside."

"It's Mayfield property, Ben, so we wouldn't be trespassing," Moki added with a smile.

"I say let's go for it," Gracie replied, speaking for her brother. She and the other girls had just come from the side of the cabin.

Ben agreed, too, and the group proceeded to the window.

After some time pounding around all sides of the window's rotted casement, Lanny was able to get the stubborn, old frame to rattle. He pressed his widespread fingers against the center of the glass and gently rocked the pane. "I think it's starting to give," he said.

"Careful, bro," said Moki. "If it breaks, our visit won't be a secret any longer."

"And my fingers won't be in too good of shape, either," Lanny replied.

A few seconds later, the window started sliding upwards Then, pop! It yielded. "Yay!" Lanny shouted, and the others cheered. "Let's go," he said as he reached inside and rolled the rotted calico curtain up over its rod.

"Here, climb on my back," Moki said as he knelt on all fours, making a table with his body. One by one, starting with Rani, the other five obliged him, putting as little pressure on the boy's back as possible. In no time, each helped the next squirm headfirst through the window with little effort.

Then, it was Moki's turn. First, however, he wisely found a large rock to put below the window to help when they got out. Next, standing on the rock and putting his hands on top of the thick casement, he used his strength to scramble up until he was sitting on the windowsill. Cheered on by his friends, he twisted and maneuvered onto his stomach. In this position, it was easy for him to slide feet first into the cabin. Fortunately, he ducked a split second before he would have hit his head on the window. Then, everyone turned to inspect the one-room building.

Ben and Gracie stood momentarily mesmerized by being inside Papa's cabin. The rest got busy looking around, still slapping the clingy shed dust off themselves. No one was surprised that there were few cobwebs in the cabin since it had obviously been used by the looters.

In the dwindling light, they saw heavy-duty cardboard boxes scattered everywhere on tables and all around the floor. Some were empty, but others contained dark-colored rocks of various sizes. Lanny turned to one of the boxes and reached for a rock with glistening gold specks. It felt like a lead weight.

"I'd say we've found some of the recently looted gold ore," Lanny announced.

"How can you be sure it's gold and not iron pyrite—fool's gold?" Moki asked.

Lanny replied, "Well, by its weight for one thing, bro. And because the thieves likely put it here, so what else would it be? But let's test a piece." He reached into his knapsack and removed a small magnet, a piece of glass, a bit of unglazed tile, and a pocketknife.

He continued, "According to my research, gold doesn't scratch glass, but iron pyrite does. Real gold, unlike iron pyrite, is not magnetic. And real gold leaves a gold streak when rubbed against unglazed ceramic, but iron pyrite leaves a green-black streak."

With the pocketknife, Lanny dug out a chunk of the golden metal from a rock. He rubbed it against the glass first, then the tile. Rani looked on with interest.

"See? The glass isn't scratched, and there is a gold streak on the tile." Lanny further proved it was gold when his magnet didn't show any attraction to the gleaming mineral.

Moki slapped his friend on the back. "Brilliant, bro. Good thing you brought that field test kit. I'm tempted to say I'll never tease you again about your habit of being overly prepared, but you and I both know that's a promise I couldn't keep."

Lanny jabbed at Moki's head in fun, which his friend successfully dodged.

Lexi called out to the group, "Hey, guys, come look at what else these boxes contain."

Everyone surrounded her by a back wall piled with at least a dozen boxes, heavy with ore. Gracie was quick to point out the containers had obviously come from Cody's general store, according to the stamp on the sides of the boxes.

Lexi replied, "That's valuable information, Gracie. Now, check out what's scrawled across the lids in red marker pen. All these boxes in this section say, 'To R.F. 10/30.'"

"Rainbow Flats," the kids said in unison as they looked from face to face.

"And 10/30—October thirtieth—that's today!" Rani said.

Moki said, "If that's true, then the thieves might show up here at any minute for the loot. I say we need to get out of here, *wiki-wiki*!"

But it was too late. The kids' joy from a day of incredible discoveries had turned to terror. A male voice was shouting to them from far below the cabin, probably near the mine.

"Kids," he said. "Wherever you are, come on out. We know you're around here. We have your horses."

CHAPTER TWENTY-TWO

· ✧ ·

At the End of the Rainbow

As soon as they heard the man's voice, Moki grabbed a box and shouted, "OMG! Barricade the door and window!"

The kids all leaped to their feet to pitch in. They knew they were probably in grave danger from one or more looters. The terrain around the cabin was unknown to them, but not to the person below, and he had their horses. Eventually, they would have to climb down, but he would probably find them before that. Still, they weren't ready to give up.

Lexi struggled with a heavy box. "But if there's only one of them—oof!"—she dropped the box in front of the door—"maybe we can overpower him?"

Rani easily hefted her box. "Maybe it's the Phantom Rider himself returning for the boxes marked 10/30." She set the box on top of Lexi's and rushed back for another. Moki and Lanny had busied themselves with piling up boxes on a table in front of the window.

Gracie's lip was quivering. "But I heard him say 'we.' There must be at least two." Suddenly, Gracie wasn't so thrilled about being a detective.

Ben said, "Guys, wait. Don't block both our escape routes. I have my cell phone—maybe it will work for a change. We're up high enough. Let's try calling my parents."

Rani stood mid-lift, two boxes in her hands this time. She didn't look convinced about not barricading.

Ben pulled his phone from his pocket, but before he could enter the number, it rang. He checked the screen. "Hey, it's my mom! Mom, Mom, I was about to call you. Come quickly. We're on the mountain in Papa's cabin, but someone has our horses and is trying to get us."

"That 'someone,' young man, is your dad and I," she replied in her usual level tone. "Goodness. Didn't you recognize your father's voice? It's four-thirty. When you didn't come home, we came looking for you as we said we would. Are all of you together and all right?"

Ben started laughing almost hysterically. It was all he could do to tell the other kids there was no danger after all. Then, seeing his friends' puzzled faces, he explained more coherently.

The five kids surrounded Ben and shouted into the phone that they were glad for the rescue. Then, Ben told his mother they were indeed safe now and on the hill above where his parents were. He asked her to watch for them. They were coming down and had some interesting things to show them.

Moki, Rani, and Lanny shoved the barricade away from the window. Then, all six clambered out more easily than they had entered, glad for Moki's mini boulder below the window for support. In less than a minute, they were waving to the Mayfield parents from the edge of the cliff. They started the descent to the rock ledge, where Rani had first seen the funicular protruding from the hole, in order to guide the adults back up to the cabin. Minutes later, everyone was hugging and reassuring Mr. and Mrs. Mayfield that they were fine.

Within an hour, Ben and Gracie's now happy and impressed parents had seen the funicular, the cabin with its stockpile of gold ore, the mine entrance and doors, and the shed with its stashed mining gear.

"You kids have done an incredible job," Mr. Mayfield said as they returned to their horses. "This is beyond my wildest dreams. We're so proud of all of you. And grateful. Imagine, Papa's mine *and* his cabin, found at last. And today before the ore could be removed. Thank you so much for this gift to our family."

"You're welcome, but there's a lot more work to do," Lanny reminded him. "We have to stop the looting that I'm certain will continue tonight, given the date on those boxes."

"Not to mention capture the entire gang of mine looters," Lexi replied.

"And we still have to unmask the Phantom Rider," Ben added. He would be glad to sleep peacefully once he knew there wasn't a phantom galloping below his window in the dead of night.

"Did the sheriff or deputy ever turn up here today to help?" Mrs. Mayfield asked.

Rani cocked her head. "Come to think of it, no."

"Well, then, it's high time I called them," Mrs. Mayfield replied. She stepped aside to try to call. Her husband wanted to call the ranch house to report they had found the kids. Both got through.

"I talked to Aunt Maisie," Mr. Mayfield reported back. "Told her and Uncle Rocky not to hold dinner for us."

"Yes, Lion and Cat need to eat," his wife agreed, putting her phone back into her pocket. "Those two kids have been working hard in the kitchen—and loving it, I can tell. As for my call, the sheriff said he would leave word for the deputy to stake out the cabin. He says there's a little-traveled emergency access road from Cody into the woods nearby, so the deputy should have no trouble finding Papa's cabin."

"Is the sheriff coming here?" Gracie asked.

"No, he and the deputy got sidetracked today and have to finish something they're doing. But he promised to meet us in Rainbow Flats soon. So, let's go." She headed her horse back to the trail the kids had used earlier in the day.

Rani pointed in the opposite direction. "Wouldn't it be faster to use the Phantom's trail by the shed to get to Rainbow Flats?"

"Brilliant, Rani," Mr. Mayfield replied. "That way, we might even beat the sheriff there."

"Yee-haw!" Lanny hollered, startling everyone. "What a day!"

They all laughed at the young boy's enthusiasm and mounted their horses. Lexi gave her brother a wink and a smile.

If the Phantom Rider had been near the shed in those next few minutes, he would have spied eight riders using his well-worn path, no longer a secret now, to cross the desert to Rainbow Flats. And he probably would have been very angry.

Dusk brought orange and purple shadows across the desert landscape as the group galloped on to the ghost town. The cacti looked like giant sentinels with arms raised, warning them to turn back. None of the determined riders knew what they would find once they arrived in Rainbow Flats but hoped the sheriff wouldn't be too far behind. The moon hadn't risen yet to light their way. Nonetheless, within an hour, they were once again approaching Main Street.

"It's almost as if this place is becoming one of our old haunts," Moki said.

"Ha. Very funny," Lanny replied with a sideways glance at his friend.

Lexi pointed ahead and said softly, "Look. I see a truck."

Ben said, "Yeah, it's at the church. No people around, though." He glanced at his sister.

Gracie groaned. "Not the church again. I was hoping never to go back there."

Rani offered, "Well, that's probably where they've stashed some boxes of gold ore."

"And the truck is probably how they get it in and out of here," Moki said.

"I'm guessing the thieves are inside, getting ready to load," Lanny said. "We can't risk being seen yet. Let's get off Main Street now."

Everyone agreed and veered off as quietly as possible to the right to follow the boy behind the livery stable and other buildings. From there, they could safely approach the church. Within a minute, they were two buildings away.

"Let's wait here for the sheriff," Moki said. "We should be careful—in case we need him or his warrant to raid the place."

Soon, Gracie looked over and noticed Ginger no longer had a mount. As usual, curious Rani had slipped away and headed directly for the church. Mrs. Mayfield was about to protest when the girl returned.

"Sorry. I took a peek through one of the church windows. There are four people inside—three men and one woman. I didn't recognize any of them since their backs were to me. They're shuffling what look like ore boxes toward the door. The good news is I didn't see anything resembling weapons."

"Betcha Rufus would have been person number five if he wasn't already in jail," Gracie said through partially pursed lips.

"There could be even more than five in the ring," Mrs.

Mayfield whispered. "Oh, I hope the sheriff gets here in time. And Gracie, I don't want you going inside that church if it becomes necessary for the rest of us to go in."

"But Mom, I don't want to miss out on nabbing the crooks!"

Her mother smiled, shook her head, and leaned over to stroke her daughter's hair.

Ben bit his lip. "I hope beyond hope that one of the guys in there is the Phantom Rider."

Within minutes, which seemed like hours to the group, Sheriff Buckley arrived. He slowly pulled in, saw the truck, turned off his car's headlights, and rolled quietly right up Main Street to the church. Lanny had been watching for him and now signaled to the group. The riders dismounted and joined the sheriff next to his car without a sound. The thieves must have been too busy to notice what was happening outside.

Lexi enjoyed learning detection methods from the police, so she whispered, "Sheriff, how will you get them to come out?"

"I don't plan to. I'm going in. I want to surprise them. We can't risk their running out the back door if there is one."

"Cool," Lexi replied. "What can the rest of us do to help?"

"Go let the air out of all the truck's tires. Then, everyone, wait out here until I signal you."

The six kids had to stifle laughs as they unscrewed and pressed on the tires' air valve pins. This time, the hissing sound Moki heard was only the tires going flat.

Soon, everyone huddled by the sheriff's car and watched the lawman bravely walk up to the front door. He opened it noiselessly and, unseen, stood with his hands on his hips and watched the thieves at their work for a few more seconds.

"Well, I'll be," he finally said loudly. "Annie Banks! And Nate Seeley, too? What do you think you're doing?"

Annie Banks, Cody's general store owner, and Nate Seeley, Cody Café's head cook, froze immediately and almost dropped the large chunks of gold ore from their hands onto their feet. They stared at the sheriff, then at their two partners who were farther back in the church. One of the remaining two men bolted past the sheriff and jumped into the truck. Between the dark desert night and his haste, he hadn't noticed the four flats.

The kids ran to the truck's cab door. "Neat trick, huh?" Moki said as they opened the door, laughing. The man got out without a fight but gave a deep groan when he saw the tires.

Mr. Mayfield faced him. "What? Jed Hollister? You were in on this caper, too? I don't understand you. We've been neighbors and friends for years. I'm beyond shocked."

Jed hung his head but said nothing. Mrs. Mayfield restrained herself in front of the kids. Her only comment was to glare intensely at their former friend, who hung his head even lower.

The sheriff emerged from the church with Banks and Seeley, then took Hollister into custody as well. All three were handcuffed and read their rights.

While the sheriff was busy, the kids quickly slipped into the church to flush out the fourth looter, hoping the lawman and the Mayfield parents wouldn't see them. Their plan worked.

Ben's eyes scanned the room. He grinned, then called out, "No sense in trying to hide. We see you up there in the dark choir loft. There's no way out. Come on down, Mr. Wells."

Parker Wells said some angry words that were thankfully unintelligible. But he soon complied, storming down the stairs two at a time. He resisted doing or saying anything else foolish to the kids when he saw the sheriff and the Mayfield parents standing in the doorway.

Rani couldn't help asking, "Mr. Wells, what was that you said about Papa's gold mine no longer producing?"

The man's only response was to glower menacingly at the girl, which didn't bother her in the least.

The sheriff immediately crossed the room, shook his head, and said to the assayer, "And Parker. You, too? I can't believe it. I always thought of you as one of Cody's most upstanding citizens."

Once the lawman recovered from the shock, he read the fourth looter his rights and led him in handcuffs out to the police car. It was a tight squeeze, but the sheriff managed to secure all of them in the back seat.

"I suggest all of you get attorneys once I have you back in Cody," the sheriff told them. "I'm charging each of you with grand theft pertaining to the gold mine, not to mention trespassing on the Mayfields' property. You can bet we'll be discussing how much ore you've already transported out of the area. And, no doubt, there will be more charges coming, such as stealing from the Mayfield ranch house grounds."

All four instantly denied being on or taking anything from the ranch house area.

The sheriff said, "Well, we already have your confederate, Rufus Crawford, in custody. So, then. Maybe there's at least one more of you—called 'The Man' if I'm not mistaken?" He waited for a response, as did Ben, who was anxious to learn who the Phantom Rider really was.

Parker Wells was the only one of the four prisoners with the wherewithal to speak. With a sneer, he said, "I can tell you for a fact, sheriff, you haven't caught the whole gang yet. But I won't be the one to rat." He turned and eyed the other captives threateningly.

Just then, Ned Buchanan arrived, his police car screeching to a halt by the group.

When he approached the others, Lexi smiled at him and said, "Yay, more help."

The deputy doffed his hat to her, then turned to the sheriff. "By the time I got to the cabin, it had been cleaned out. The gang must have beaten me there and taken the ore boxes. So, I decided to come here. How can I help?"

Sheriff Buckley thanked the deputy and asked him to proceed to Cody's jail with the prisoners while he, the Mayfields, and the detectives searched for more boxes inside the church. The deputy exchanged cars with the sheriff and immediately drove off with the four looters. The remaining lawman secured the truck already filled with boxes, and the group went into the building again.

Once inside, Lanny said, "I'm guessing the church was the looters' main staging area before transporting the ore out."

The sheriff nodded. "Time will tell from our search."

Lexi replied, "Yeah, and with the Phantom stationed here in town as the ores' nighttime guard. But we didn't see the boxes when we caught Rufus here the other night, so they must have been brought in afterwards and hidden someplace."

"I think you're right," Gracie called from the sacristy, a room just off the altar. The group followed her voice. "Come see. This is where the reverend must have kept church candles and things years ago. Just look at all these boxes of ore in here. And yuck, lots of spiders, too."

"How about snakes?" Moki asked as he peeked around the corner into the room.

"No snakes, bro," Lanny said. "Just one big chicken— if you come in."

"Ha, ha. Good one, bro," Moki replied and entered the little room.

"I wonder where they take it and how long they've been transporting it," Rani said.

Lanny said, "And if the ore was cleared out of the cabin, as Deputy Buchanan said it was, "where is it now?"

"Well," Lexi replied, "it certainly wasn't brought here since we arrived."

"Right, BFF, because no one could have beaten us here with it," Rani added.

"So, we won't find any boxes labeled '10/30' in the truck or inside the church," Moki said.

"Not unless some other boxes with that same label were brought earlier," Lanny replied.

The sheriff said, "We'll be conducting a thorough investigation including a search of this entire town. We'll find the answers to your questions, kids. And I'll bet you one of the jailed looters cracks under pressure by morning. But I doubt we would have ever uncovered this ring or its shenanigans, let alone caught any of them, if it hadn't been for you six brave kids."

Moki replied, "Thanks, but uh, sheriff? May I make a suggestion? When you search the town, avoid the saloon. But if you must look there, don't look behind the player piano."

Lanny snickered and told the puzzled sheriff he would explain later. The sheriff merely shrugged.

Then Moki started laughing and added, "Hey, I thought of something. We found gold . . . at the end of the rainbow—Rainbow Flats, that is." It didn't take much for the search-weary group to appreciate Moki's humor.

Lanny finished chuckling and said, "Beyond gold, let's hope the Rainbow Flats prisoners crack for the sheriff by tomorrow. Oh, and speaking of cracking, bro, I love it when you crack yourself up."

"And, apparently, when I crack you up, too."

CHAPTER TWENTY-THREE

· ✧ ·

Spooky Moonlight

Everyone was gathered around the ranch's kitchen counters piled high with party treats for the next night's Halloween barn dance and farewell party. It was eight o'clock, and the kids were finally feeling the effects of their long day on the mountaintop. They'd found Papa's long-lost mine and shut down a gold-looting ring, or at least part of it. They were tired, proud, and *hungry*.

"Make it *two* sloppy joes, Uncle Rocky," Ben declared as Rocky, Lionel, and Catherine handed dinner plates to the dusty detectives. "Feels like a year since I ate anything."

"I'll match you bite for bite, dude." Moki rubbed his growling belly and loaded his plate with hash browns and three scoops of green salad in addition to sloppy joes.

The rest of the riders, their plates similarly piled high, regaled Lionel, Catherine, and the two cooks with tales of capturing bad guys and boxes of gold.

"Wow," said Catherine with a frown. "Sorry I missed

it. But I'm even sorrier you have been victims of robbers. You're all too nice for that to have happened to you." She walked over to Mrs. Mayfield and hugged her.

Lionel shook his head. "Man, criminals are the worst, no matter who they hurt."

Catherine slowly turned to Lionel. After a brief pause, she frowned and said, "You're right, Lion." She faced the rest of the room. "I have to admit something. I'm a criminal. Or I was, anyway. I shoplifted in a department store. Some hair clips and kids' jewelry. At the time, I was only sorry I got caught, but not that I did it."

Lionel cleared his throat. "Me too. I mean, the being a criminal part. I didn't shoplift. I broke into a garage and stole a kid's electric bike. And I didn't once think about how he'd feel. I almost landed in a juvenile jail—but ended up here instead . . . thank goodness."

Rani said, "This ranch is certainly a great place to learn valuable lessons. I think all of us have."

"Yeah," Lionel replied. "I never thought about how a crime affects the victim. But I will now, and I'll remember how stealing has affected the Mayfields. I promise I'll never steal again. And you know what? I'm going to have my friends start calling me 'Lionel' again, not Lion. I don't need to pretend to be ferocious anymore. That seems like baby stuff. I couldn't even scare that mountain lioness—a *real* lion—but she sure scared me."

"No more stealing for me, either," Catherine said. She put her hand on her heart. "I promise. No, I promise me."

Everyone clapped, with the loudest applause coming from Aunt Maisie and Uncle Rocky. They had enjoyed the day baking with the two helpful kids who had made remarkable turnarounds.

"So, both of you can go home on Sunday, and I can tell your moms you're making a fresh start, right?" Mrs. Mayfield asked.

"Right!" both answered with huge smiles.

"But can we still come back here, even if we turn good?" Catherine wanted to know.

Mr. Mayfield chuckled and replied, "Of course. You're now official Youth Saddle Club members, so you can come back any weekend when we're here for as long as you want. You four detectives, too. Watch your email for special invites."

A resounding "yippee" echoed through the kitchen, also overflowing with delicious aromas of party cookies, cakes, and brownies.

Then, Mrs. Mayfield reminded Catherine and Lionel it was time for bed. "Tomorrow, you two could spend some time learning how to jump over the hurdles since you didn't get to do that today."

"Plus, some time to help decorate the barn for Halloween?" Catherine asked.

Mrs. Mayfield nodded.

She thanked everyone for all they had done that day— the kids for their fabulous work, and the two kitchen cooks for freeing her and her husband for ranch business. "I almost forgot. Everyone will get to meet our new hired hand tomorrow. Her name is Amalia Gomez. She's coming to the party."

After the cheers, Mr. Mayfield told the six remaining kids, "Now, don't stay up too late. There are lots of barn chores to do tomorrow. And the sheriff may want to talk with you some more."

"Don't worry, Dad," Ben replied. "What a day. I'm beat." He tried to disguise his heartfelt disappointment that the Phantom Rider was still at large.

Mr. and Mrs. Mayfield then said good night and led the saddle club kids to the bunkhouse.

"Hey, wait," Uncle Rocky said. "Who's going to help us bag up all these party cookies?"

"Mmm," Moki said. "Suddenly, I don't feel so sleepy. I'll help."

Lexi said, "Still predictable, Moki. Just make sure more cookies get into bags than into your stomach."

Aunt Maisie set a box of plastic bags on the counter, and the remaining six kids joined in the fun. Time passed quickly as they worked and shared more stories with the adults about the day's adventures.

A while later, five of the detectives were still bagging and nibbling on cookies while Lanny sat distracted, deep in thought. With a furrowed brow, he stared straight ahead at the kitchen wall. He felt there were more loose ends about the roundup of the criminals in Rainbow Flats. But he couldn't figure out what.

Everyone was so focused on their tasks that they didn't hear the kitchen wall clock softly chiming ten or the squeaking of the back porch screen door. In seconds, they had unexpected company. It nudged Ben in the back.

"Cookie!" shouted Ben as he jumped. "You almost gave me a heart attack. What do you think you're doing in here?"

Gracie started laughing. "Again? Oh, Cookie, you can smell cookies a mile off, can't you? I guess I was so tired when we got back, I didn't tie you up very well in the barn."

Aunt Maisie wasn't as amused. "Get that horse out of my kitchen this instant," she said, wagging her finger at the horse. Uncle Rocky, however, doubled over, laughing.

"Okay, girl, come on," Gracie said sadly. "I'll bring you a cookie in the morning."

The kids teamed up and began playfully pushing on Cookie. She started slowly moving in reverse out of the kitchen, into the back service porch, and finally, onto the stoop where Gracie could easily guide her mount back to the barn.

Despite the full moon, Ben flicked on the stoop's light for his sister. "Hurry up, Gracie. There're still lots of cookies to bag, and we have to go to bed soon."

Gracie shouted over her shoulder, "I know. I'll be right back. And you better not eat my share of the goodies."

Girl and horse crossed the yard. One at a time, the barn doors were creaked open.

Gracie decided to use the plentiful moonlight instead

of the barn's overhead lights so as not to disturb the other horses. "Don't forget. A cookie for my Cookie tomorrow," she whispered in her horse's ear.

They were almost at Cookie's stall when Gracie sensed something. Was that a soft neigh she had heard from the back of the barn? There weren't supposed to be any horses there.

Gracie gulped. "Is someone else in here?" No one answered. Her mind instantly raced back to the other barn incident that resulted in her kidnapping. She wanted to retreat. *If only I could get to the light switch*, she thought, chiding herself for not turning it on in the first place. But Cookie wasn't in her stall yet, so Gracie's path was blocked. And the switch panel was too far away. She froze and listened.

Slowly and almost noiselessly, something emerged from deep in the barn. Then, its clip-clop told Gracie it was a horse. Her eyes had adjusted to the darkness, and the moonlight revealed it—a large white horse. Lightning! But where was its rider? The Phantom had to be near. She shivered as she gazed all around.

Gracie felt beads of cold perspiration dapple her forehead and upper lip, the hairs on her arms rise, and surfacing goosebumps tingle. She opened her mouth, only to discover her voice had fled, just as it had when Rufus had confronted her. But this time, it wasn't afternoon. Darkness engulfed the barn, intensifying her fear. The lump in her throat felt like a rock.

Gracie startled. *What's that?* A bright patch of moonlight had revealed something glowing for a split second near the white horse. *The Phantom Rider's eyes! He's close. Too close.* But the rest of him remained invisible in the darkness.

Suddenly, a high-pitched voice in the vicinity of the glowing eyes shrieked, causing Gracie to jump and grab firmly ahold of Cookie's mane. "Get out! Leave this ranch, or I will harm it and your family. And I will start with you!"

The voice, obviously distorted by a device, was like something from another planet. Then, it hit Gracie. Had the Phantom Rider let Cookie out purposely to lure her to the barn? But what would he do next? What should she do next?

Not waiting any longer, Grace jerked on Cookie's mane, rapidly turning the horse toward the door. "Not on your life!" she yelled over her shoulder, keeping her eyes on the escape route. *If only we could get outside, Cookie and I would be safe*, she thought.

Just as she and her horse reached the doors, however, Lightning burst upon them, hooves flailing. She could clearly see the Phantom in the saddle now, holding the reins high, spurring his horse onward.

Ben and the four detectives had just come outside to look for Gracie. They heard the commotion as one barn door flew wide open. Gracie charged out and instantly let go of Cookie.

"Help!" she yelled, her arms stretched out before her as she hightailed it to the stoop, glad to see the others. The Phantom Rider and Lightning made a beeline for the group.

The strange scene completely unnerved Cookie. Now left to her own devices, she thrashed around the intruders, giving the kids a few blessed seconds to figure out what was happening.

"Aww!" yelled Ben from the stoop. "Not you again. Show your face or leave, coward." But his words weren't needed.

Rider and horse had been caught off guard. Lightning reared up to avoid being side-bumped by Cookie. But the confusion was more than the white horse could endure.

"Whoa, Lightning, whoa," the Phantom shouted. It was no good. Lightning had his own plans to save himself. Once his front hooves hit the ground, the horse bucked hard.

The Phantom's feet flew out of his stirrups, and he soared out of the saddle, landing hard on the ground with a resounding "oof." In a white streak, the horse sped off into the night, hooves pounding, past the barn and bunkhouse, into the far meadow, and was swallowed up in the moonlit landscape.

The Phantom, however, couldn't escape this time. He had been knocked out and lay sprawled on the ground. His black hat rested several yards away against a tree. The small, hand-held voice device the Phantom had used to frighten Gracie was shattered into many blue plastic pieces nearby.

The older kids ran to the downed man to check for injuries. Fortunately, he was still breathing, and he had only a few minor scrapes on his chest. Lanny decided to err on the side of caution, so he pulled out his cell phone and dialed 9-1-1.

Gracie thought fast and ran into the back service porch, returning with two pieces of rope as Aunt Maisie and Uncle Rocky looked on in confusion. Lexi, Moki, and Rani gently pulled the Phantom's hands toward his back and tied him securely. Next, they tied his feet.

"Yay. This time, the spook's been spooked," Lanny said. "Quick, Ben. Unmask him before the paramedics get here!"

"With pleasure." Ben stooped, not believing their good luck, and pulled carefully on the black ski mask, watching for possible injuries. Despite it being tight, the disguise soon peeled off into his hands. Everyone gathered around the unconscious man to see who had been terrorizing them and stealing from the ranch.

The backyard stoop light was dim, but the moonlight aided them. There could be no mistake about whom they saw lying captive in the Mayfields' back yard. Audible gasps echoed from the group.

"If Sheriff Buckley was shocked to learn who the looters were earlier this evening, imagine what he'll say when he gets a load of this guy," Ben said.

The kids were staring down at a former lawman. Deputy Ned Buchanan.

CHAPTER TWENTY-FOUR

· ✧ ·

Tough Lessons

Gracie, Ben, and the four detectives slept fitfully that Friday night. The initial exhilaration over the Phantom Rider's capture and unmasking was soon replaced with anguish over a powerful sense of loss. It had been disturbing to see a man taken away in an ambulance, criminal or not. He had regained consciousness before he left, and the paramedics said he'd be fine soon enough. But it was still bad all around.

Many people had been hurt by the looters' crimes and activities. The kids' sweet dreams of solving the case by finding Papa's gold mine and cabin had been soured by startling experiences. Gracie's kidnapping. Rushing bats. Slithering snakes. A wild gallop across the desert to a ghost town. The capture of the astonishing looters, all Cody citizens who had been friendly over the years with the Mayfields. And the Phantom's final, unexpected terrifying visit to the Mayfields' barn and yard, flashing red lights and all.

Whatever the reason for Ned Buchanan's foolish, last ride—greed, anger, or revenge—his actions had already cost him dearly. He would be trading his badge for prison. The former deputy and his confederates had lost the trust and respect of all their neighbors, the sheriff, the detectives, and especially the Mayfields. In addition to forfeiting their freedom, the looters would never realize any of the wealth they had hungrily anticipated from all their hard, illegal work mining and transporting the stolen gold ore.

No wonder moods were subdued Saturday morning at the breakfast table. Catherine and Lionel seemed to be the only ones who welcomed the wonderful meal of scrambled eggs, crispy bacon, and Uncle Rocky's famous chocolate chip–pumpkin bread. Grief has a way of erasing hunger.

Aunt Maisie's was the cold voice of reason. "Okay, everybody. Time to snap out of it. What's done is done. Let's all take a deep breath, hold up our heads, smile, and move forward. We aren't the ones behind bars, after all. Much good often comes from bad. You'll see."

"Plus, it's Halloween," Uncle Rocky added. "Didn't any of you notice the incredibly wonderful decorations Aunt Maisie and I put up extra early this morning?"

No one had.

Above their heads, festooning the chandelier, they now noticed black and orange balloons. Twisted papier-maché streamers in the same holiday colors draped from the dining room's four corners and trailed downward from the center of the light fixture.

"And think about how rich all you Mayfields will be when that bundle of gold ore is found," Lionel said while helping himself to more bacon.

Swallowing a mouthful of egg, Catherine added, "And more gold to come from your Papa's mine."

Mr. Mayfield was the first of the gloomy group to speak. "Hmm . . . I can't say as though I'd thought much about that." His eyebrows were raised as he slowly nodded his head and looked toward his wife.

Her face was still cupped in her hands. "But look at the price we pay for it. So many people deceived us . . . long-time neighbors and friends we entertained right here in this house, at this table, or did business with in town. Annie Banks from the general store, the café's cook, Nate Seeley, and our friend and neighbor, Jed Hollister. Oh dear, and what's to become of poor Emma Hollister now that Jed's in jail? And then there's former Deputy Buchanan . . ."

Lionel interrupted, "Well, as Jax would say, 'Life's often full of disappointment.'"

Catherine added, "Yes, and he also says, 'Life's full of surprises—some good, some bad. You gotta take whatever comes and move on.'"

Suddenly, Mrs. Mayfield lifted her head and slowly laughed. "Well, so now who are the teachers, and who are the students? Thanks. You two kids are the best."

The saddle club members beamed.

Mrs. Mayfield continued, addressing her kids and the detectives, "And how self-centered of me. You kids have solved your case! The mysteries of Papa's mine and the Phantom are history."

"Thanks for the opportunity. We had a blast," Lanny said as the squad nodded in agreement. "And we couldn't have done it without Ben and Gracie."

The two siblings smiled ear to ear.

"Hurray," Uncle Rocky said, lifting his arms high as if he was signaling a touchdown. "So, let's eat. Everything's getting cold."

"Okay, I'll start," Moki said. He quickly snatched the thickest slice of pumpkin bread from the nearby platter.

"Moki, you're still predictable," Lexi replied, "but this morning, that's fab."

"Oh . . . the Halloween party's tonight. I almost forgot," Gracie said sitting bolt upright. "Gosh, we have so much decorating to do. And I still need to finish my costume."

"And don't forget about those dozen or so pumpkins on the back porch," Aunt Maisie added. "Lots of helpers will be needed to turn them into jack-o'-lanterns."

"Then let's have a pumpkin carving contest," Rani said with a welcomed, perky tone.

Lanny replied, "You're on." He was glad they would have some fun distractions as they awaited Sheriff Buckley's promised arrival later that morning with more news about the case.

"I already know what I'm going to carve," Ben said. But no matter how much he was begged, he wouldn't tell.

"Just wait and see. Maybe it'll be one of life's *good* surprises."

As they finished breakfast, Moki reminded everyone, "If it hadn't been for Grandma's sneezing and those rushing bats, we might not have found Papa's gold mine."

Gracie added, "Right. And if it hadn't been for Cookie coming into the kitchen last night—whether or not the Phantom released her to coax me into the barn—he might still be riding. Ha!"

Even Aunt Maisie had to concede Gracie's point.

"Three cheers for the horses," Lanny said.

And everyone shouted, "Hip, hip, hooray for horses!"

CHAPTER TWENTY-FIVE

· ◇ ·

Halloween Barn Dance

Breakfast was soon finished and cleared away. The discussion during the meal had been intense. Now, it was time for some fun. Catherine and Lionel went to the arena with Mr. and Mrs. Mayfield to jump some low hurdles. The other six kids helped with the dishes, so the kitchen could be turned quickly into their pumpkin-carving station. Newspapers were spread over the countertops, and each claimed their spot for designing two jack-o'-lanterns apiece. The gooey pumpkin innards were soon disposed of, and the fun carving work lay before them.

In no time, a motley assortment of jack-o'-lanterns grinned at the contestants, who had lined them up in a long row for judging. Some had friendly, toothy smiles while others sported jagged teeth and scary, contorted mouths and eyes. But none was as captivating as Ben's, which won unanimously, even garnering Aunt Maisie's and Uncle Rocky's votes.

"Wow, those are incredible silhouettes of the Phantom

Rider and Lightning," Rani said to Ben. "I'd say you're destined to be an artist someday, Ben."

"Thanks. Maybe as a hobby," he replied. "I really want to be a deputy marshal."

Lexi added, "Well, I'd say you just made your first arrest—the Phantom, imprisoned in a pumpkin."

The kids placed candles inside their creations and lit them. Then they flicked off the kitchen lights to test the gruesome effect.

Later that morning, all the kids and adults were busy decorating the barn for the Halloween party. Moki had finished his famous coconut-pineapple upside-down cake for the event. Catherine and Lionel were occupied making popcorn strings, but they ate more than they strung.

Lanny said, "Can you guys believe it was only one week ago today we accepted our case at the Mayfields' Walnut Street barbecue?" The others shook their heads.

Sheriff Buckley arrived around eleven. He talked as he pitched in, helping Mr. Mayfield and Jax jiggle hay bales into position to mark off the perimeter of the dance floor.

As the sheriff had predicted, nearly all the prisoners had volunteered to talk in the hope of reducing their certain prison time. Ned Buchanan and Parker Wells were the only holdouts. The other four reported the deputy had been the ringleader with the assayer second in command. Buchanan, Wells, Annie Banks, Jed Hollister, Nate Seeley, and Rufus

Crawford had comprised the entire gang. They confirmed that they had mined in secret by night on the mountainside, using the lights from the shed to do their unlawful work.

Lanny finally figured out what was bothering him about the roundup of the thieves at Rainbow Flats. "Sheriff, were the ore boxes really cleared out of Papa's cabin as the deputy had said?"

"Not entirely. I found a few in the trunk of his police car. The rest were still in the cabin. Ned had indeed gone to the cabin, but not to stake it out. He was there to collect ore boxes and was bringing some to Rainbow Flats. When he saw me already there, he apparently played his part as deputy, not revealing his hidden stash. His confederates kept his secrets—until this morning. Must have been difficult for him to trade cars with me."

Lanny said. "No doubt! He had to leave his gold ore with you last night and worry about you finding it. All of us had assumed he told us the truth about those cabin boxes."

"But he didn't," said Rani. "Wow, there must have been some interesting conversations between the deputy and his partners in crime on two occasions. The first was when the deputy took Rufus into custody the other night. The second was last night when he drove the other four to jail—and without the ore boxes."

"Golly, I imagine you're right," said the sheriff. "Rufus confessed he had tied up Gracie briefly in the church so he could get the ski mask from Ned's room in the hotel. He had hidden it inside his jacket. Fortunately for us, he didn't know where the claim document was and counted on Ned arriving to retrieve it. Instead, all of us got there first. Rufus said Ned almost stopped to get the paper before driving back to Cody. But it was too risky with all of you and me so close by. Rufus gave Ned the ski mask once they were in the car. Ned had planned to return to get the claim paper, then sleep."

"Lucky for us about the claim document still being there," Lexi said as she propped up a huge spray of autumn flowers. "And it does explain why the ski mask was missing when we searched the Phantom's hotel room closet right after Ned took Rufus to jail. You know, his getting that mask back led to his last ride and capture."

The sheriff confirmed the deputy had become the Phantom Rider to scare the Mayfields into selling their property, so the gang could continue looting the gold indefinitely. He also stated that Ned Buchanan did admit to intentionally releasing Gracie's horse to lure the girl to the dark barn to frighten her.

"And could his final ride last night have been because he was angry at us kids for shutting down their gold-looting operation?" Ben asked.

"That's what Jed Hollister said," the sheriff replied. "And, I imagine, out of revenge. No telling what he might have done in anger if you kids and Cookie hadn't stopped him."

"Which reminds me," Ben said. He excused himself and ran to the house. Soon, he returned with the Phantom's black ski mask and proudly handed it to the sheriff.

As Moki hung up strands of Halloween lights, he

asked, "But where did they take the gold ore, and how long has their operation been going on?"

"They mostly used that same truck and the emergency access road to get it from the cabin to Rainbow Flats. Sometimes, Ned would take small loads on horseback when he returned to the hotel each night after a mining episode. Then, once they had a large enough load, they would drive it in the same truck across the border into southern Nevada. According to Annie Banks, they've been doing that for the past five months."

"That's a lot of ore. Any chance of retrieving any of it?" Ben asked.

"I'm happy to report we already have. Nate Seeley told us about the warehouse in Nevada where they stashed it. They hadn't had a chance to process the gold out of it yet. So, in addition to the gang's other crimes, we can add transporting stolen goods across a state line. The Nevada police are picking it up for us today. There are literally tons of it."

"Woohoo!" shouted Gracie. "Thanks, sheriff. Now, my family's Youth Saddle Club business will be in the money forever. No more worries about that for Mom and Dad."

"Did you find out who Rufus was talking to on the phone the night Gracie heard him from the hayloft?" Jax asked from atop a nearby ladder.

"Rufus said that was Parker Wells, whose job it was to contact Ned, 'The Man,' about getting the claim document out of the hotel that night. He also confessed that Parker, being the assayer, had stolen Papa Mayfield's gold mine claim from the assay office in the first place months ago to keep any of you from finding the mine. It was apparently Ned who crafted the warning notes that had been nailed to the tack room wall, but Rufus put them there."

Jax added, "You know, I've been wondering why Rufus was so slow to get a rope from the barn to lasso that maniac's white horse the night they rode through. Now, I know why."

Lanny said to the other kids, "Ned and Parker being the leaders of the caper seems to explain why we witnessed the assayer burst into the sheriff's office that day we rode to Cody. Parker probably wanted to warn the deputy that we kids were asking questions about the mine."

"But he stopped short when he saw us and the sheriff there," Moki replied.

"I just thought of something," Lexi said. "Remember when the deputy came here to question us after we reported seeing the Phantom Rider? He even asked if any of us knew who it was, which we didn't then. He must have, first, been relieved that we hadn't recognized him, and second, been laughing at us from behind his lawman's uniform."

"Wow. That's right," Rani replied. "But *we* had the last laugh on him last night."

Mrs. Mayfield got down from a ladder. "Those criminals hurt us all, including the citizens of Cody, who will have to decide whether or not they can place their trust in their neighbors and a new deputy again. Did any of them give an explanation for why they did these terrible things?"

"Money, of course. They hoped to get rich from selling

the gold," the sheriff replied. "Their greed apparently overrode their loyalties, duties, and senses of right and wrong. In fact, the only other thing Ned said to me this morning was that he knew he would never get rich just being a deputy."

"Well, that's not true," Gracie said. "My Papa did."

Ben added, "Yeah, the honest way. With hard, law-abiding, respectful work."

"That's one of the many traits I will always admire about Papa Mayfield," said the sheriff.

Mrs. Mayfield said, "Speaking of money, after we set up a foundation to support the Youth Saddle Club for years to come and get you kids' college funds squared away, we'll have to decide which charities could best use some of our unexpected golden fortune."

She quickly turned to the four detectives, "And don't you kids worry. Mr. Mayfield and I will be talking to your parents about making sizable contributions to your college educations, too."

The kids started to protest, but she held up her hands to silence them, saying, "Now listen. We Mayfields wouldn't have this incredible bonanza if it hadn't been for all of you."

Each detective thanked her profusely, then turned back to the sheriff.

"Did anyone find Lightning?" Lexi asked. "He must still be scared and lonely."

The sheriff said, "No worries. I found him this morning, and he's fine. Guess where?"

Gracie glanced up at the ceiling, then said, "I know. In his stall . . . in Rainbow Flats!"

"You're right," he answered. "And Dr. Jameson offered to take him. He's already at her ranch living the good life with apples, carrots, greens, and a big bucket of alfalfa mash."

"That's the best news I've heard all day," Rani replied.

The sheriff added that Ned sometimes stabled Lightning and stashed his black riding outfit at Nate Seeley's ranch when he wasn't in Rainbow Flats. Then, he would pick up his police car from Seeley's to drive into Cody to work.

Gracie asked, "Say, did you find any fingerprints on the gear from the livery stable?"

"No," the sheriff said. "Ned must have used his knowledge of evidence collection procedures to ensure he didn't make any—or maybe, he rubbed them off. No matter. We have plenty of other evidence. By the way, after the looters' trials, I will be returning all that stolen gear to you Mayfields."

With that, the sheriff promised to return later for the party and left. The others got busy stringing lights and fake cobwebs and placing their jack-o'-lanterns around the barn. Then, they helped Aunt Maisie and Uncle Rocky set up and decorate long tables for food platters and the many punch bowls. By five o'clock, the barn looked fit for all the Halloween revelers who cared to stop by. And the Mayfields and the detectives had entirely shaken off the gloom they had felt that morning.

Mr. Mayfield reported that the barn phone had been ringing nonstop all day. News had already traveled all the way to Las Palmitas about the capture of the Phantom Rider and his gang and the kids' part in it. Former saddle club attendees and their families were wondering if it was too late to accept their invitations to tonight's party. Mr. Mayfield told them they were most welcome and to spread the word— the more, the merrier. So far, at least fifty families had said yes. The detectives' parents had also called with their hearty congratulations. They and Bruce would attend as well.

By seven o'clock, the barn was bursting with almost two hundred costumed partygoers. Rousing music from a local fiddlers' band was booming. Supportive neighbors had arrived with more casseroles and salads. Everyone was greeted by the glowing jack-o'-lanterns, tables of scrumptious holiday food and beverages, and the Mayfields.

Soon, the party overflowed out the barn door and into the back yard. Sheriff Buckley and his wife were dancing as were Jax and the newly hired hand, Amalia Gomez. Bruce and his girlfriend Katie were talking with Uncle Rocky and Aunt Maisie by the punch bowls. Catherine's and Lionel's mothers were beaming as their kids shared their many adventures from a fun week at the ranch. The detectives' parents were deep in conversation with Mr. and Mrs. Mayfield. Given the laughter and smiles, compliments and good news must have been resounding.

Lionel had dressed up as a lion and Catherine as a cat, both complete with whiskers and long tails. Gracie had morphed into a giant chocolate chip cookie in honor of her wandering horse. Rani was an East Indian princess, dazzling in an orange sari with golden sequins. Her arms were covered with henna tattoos, which she promised Gracie and Catherine she would paint on them tomorrow before they headed home. Lexi had transformed into Cleopatra, queen of the Nile, reflecting her desire to be an Egyptologist someday. Moki was the famous Hawaiian *paniolo* Ikua Purdy with a tall cowboy hat. Instead of a traditional cotton cowboy shirt under his vest, he had chosen a colorful, short-sleeved Hawaiian shirt. Lanny was Sherlock Holmes, complete with a tweed cape and deerstalker hat. He proudly carried his curved pipe and giant magnifying glass all evening. But Ben once again took the prize, this time with his costume. He had re-created Papa's outfit from the old photo where the dapper deputy marshal had become an equally well-dressed gold miner. The guests thought Papa himself was in attendance that night.

Aunt Maisie had dressed up like a Bohemian wanderer with a long, calico skirt, jingling bracelets, and large hoop earrings. Uncle Rocky wore a tuxedo and silk top hat. The two joined the dancers with the detectives looking on.

It was at that moment that the four started experiencing the old, empty feeling that overtook them once a case was closed. Would another mystery that needed solving come their way? If so, how long would they have to wait?

Without knowing why, Rani left the group and wandered over to the barn door. She gazed out into the darkness of the most amazing Halloween night of her life. Then, she listened carefully, focusing on the evening's stillness while trying to block out party cheer. No, she thought. It couldn't have been the Phantom Rider she had heard. . . . It must have been something else.

Soon, her three detective friends joined her.

Lanny said, "I was just thinking. Doesn't it seem that with each mystery we take on, the world gets a little smaller?"

"I think I know what you mean," Lexi replied. "Even though we started this case at a party on Walnut Street in town last weekend, here we are, way out in the country at a party in a barn. Hey! This was our first 'away' case as an official detective agency—if you don't count spending many nights in the house on Eucalyptus Street in our last mystery."

"I don't count that," said Rani, "because this time, we're definitely outside the neighborhood."

"And," Moki added, "this probably won't be our last 'away' case."

"Wait, Moki," Lexi said. "Are you hinting like last time that you already know where our next mystery is? Because if you are . . ."

"Nope," he replied. "Not a clue. But I do hope we get to cover some ground."

"I hope you're right, bro," Lanny replied, gently jostling his friend's shoulder.

If jack-o'-lanterns could speak, those in the barn might

have begun whispering to the kids, saying, "Moki's right. Your next mystery is already rumbling on Botanic Hill's Saffron Street. And get ready—because it will take you even farther from home."

Kids—thank you for buying and reading my Book 3. If you enjoyed it, I would appreciate your leaving a review online.

I'd love to hear your questions or comments, too. You can contact me at **www.sherrilljoseph.com/contact**.

You can also sign up for my monthly newsletter, geared to kids, at **https://bit.ly/3dx6L9J**. Follow the Botanic Hill detectives' interests and escapades, get a recipe, a book suggestion, and read my Dog's Blog!

And if you want to rejoin the Botanic Hill Detectives for the next adventure in the series, please watch for Book 4, *Saffron Street: Island Danger* coming in 2022. Accompany our heroes as they head to Hawai'i to try to recover an expensive, long-lost black pearl necklace. The person who might have helped them locate it dies suddenly. Another disappears. What connects the mystery to the 1941 attack on Pearl Harbor? Who is the sea cave diver who first appears in Las Palmitas but turns up in Hawai'i? Others are after the necklace, too. Can the detectives outsmart them and find it first? Get Book 4, and dare to find out!

Setting Up to Play Texas Hold 'em

A Brief History of the Game

The card game Texas hold 'em is a variation of the classic card game poker. Texas hold 'em was invented in Robstown, Texas, in the early 1900s and, in part, made famous in movies.

Important: Learn This First

Because Texas hold 'em is related to poker, you will need to learn poker's card hand rankings—in other words, what beats what. For example, a royal flush beats a straight flush. A straight flush beats four of a kind, and so on. There are ten hand rankings from one (the highest, best hand) to ten (the lowest—not the best—hand). Sound confusing? It isn't. Don't know a royal flush from a straight flush? No problem. Here is a great website to answer these questions: https://www.cardplayer.com/rules-of-poker/hand-rankings. It shows the card hand rankings from one to ten with names, descriptions, and color illustrations of the poker hands. You can even print the chart to use while you play until you know the rankings by heart.

About Betting

Betcha don't know this! Betting, which means putting down money or anything of value while playing cards, is legal in *only* nineteen states in the United States. Even in those states, the minimum age to bet during card games is between eighteen and twenty-one. Check your state's or country's laws on betting while playing any kind of poker at http://www.poker.diy.com/.

Get Set Up for Texas Hold 'em

Like poker, Texas hold 'em uses a standard card deck of fifty-two cards. Four to ten players is optimal. Add a table surrounded by chairs and some willing opponents, and you're almost set.

Now you're ready to learn the easy steps for playing Texas hold 'em poker. Log on to http://www.pokerology.com/lessons/basic-rules-of-poker/. It gives clear directions and illustrations.

On that site, you will even find the meanings of relevant terms such as *the button, small blind, big blind,* and *hole cards, the flop, the turn,* and *the river.* (Other terms like *the pot, bet, call, raise,* or *fold* won't be important to learn right now since they pertain to betting.)

Have fun!

Sources: *The information on the history of Texas hold 'em, the laws about betting when playing any form of poker, and how to set up to play the card game were paraphrased from and fact-checked using the three websites given within the piece as well as Wikipedia. All sources were active at the time of publication.*

RECIPES FROM THE RANCH

Moki's Incredible Coconut-Pineapple Upside-Down Cake (Easy Version)

1½ cups dark brown sugar, packed
¾ cups (1½ sticks) cold salted butter
1 can (20 ounces) pineapple slices, drained (save juice)
12 maraschino cherries, drained
1 to 2 cups sweetened flake coconut
1 box cake mix (2-layer size; white or yellow variety)
Eggs and oil according to cake mix directions,
    substituting saved pineapple juice for water

Preheat oven to 350°. Sprinkle brown sugar evenly in bottom of a 13" x 9" glass baking pan. Cut butter into 12 pieces; arrange evenly on top of sugar. Put pan into oven for 5–7 minutes or until the mixture is melted. Remove from oven. Stir with fork to blend. Spread evenly in pan.

Arrange drained pineapple slices neatly on top of the melted butter mixture. Place one maraschino cherry in the center of each pineapple ring. Sprinkle coconut over all. Set aside.

Make the cake mix according to package directions, substituting saved pineapple juice for the water. Add water to juice if needed. (Use your favorite "scratch" white or yellow cake recipe instead if you prefer.) Pour cake batter evenly into pan on top of fruit. Do not stir.

Bake on center rack of oven at 350° for 25 minutes. Reduce oven temperature to 325°. Bake for 15–20 minutes more or until knife inserted in center comes out clean. Remove from oven and cool in the pan on a wire rack for 30 minutes.

Slide knife around pan sides. Quickly invert pan onto a large serving tray so the fruit is now on top. Let rest for at least 30 minutes before serving. Sprinkle with more coconut.

Makes 12 big or 24 small servings. (Cake cuts better after refrigeration.)
Refrigerate leftovers.

Lexi's Fabulous Fudgy
Chocolate Brownies with Sprinkles

½ cups (1 stick) salted butter
1½ ounces unsweetened solid chocolate squares
1 teaspoon vanilla extract
2/3 cups unsweetened dark cocoa powder
1½ cups granulated sugar
2 large egg whites, lightly beaten
2 large whole eggs, lightly beaten
1¼ cups all-purpose flour
¾ teaspoon baking powder
Cooking spray or butter
Your favorite colorful sprinkles

Preheat oven to 325°. Melt butter and solid chocolate completely in a large saucepan over medium heat. Stir in vanilla extract, then cocoa powder. Cook one minute. Stir in sugar. Cook one more minute, being careful not to scorch the mixture. Remove pan from heat. Cool slightly.

Combine egg whites and whole eggs in a large mixing bowl. Gradually add warm chocolate mixture in very small portions (about 1/2 cup at a time) to egg mixture, stirring with a whisk after each addition until well-blended.

Lightly spoon flour into measuring cups and level with a knife. Combine flour and baking powder in a small mixing bowl. Stir to blend well. Add flour mixture to chocolate mixture to two portions, stirring well after each addition.

Coat bottom and sides of a 9-inch square baking pan with cooking spray or butter. Spoon batter evenly into pan. Shake on sprinkles. Bake at 325° for 27 minutes. Do not overbake.

Cool. Makes 12 large or 16 small brownies.

Rani's Favorite Old-Style Mac 'n' Cheese

2. cups (8 ounces) uncooked elbow macaroni
½ cup chopped onion
4 Tablespoons (1/2 cube) salted butter or margarine
½ teaspoon each salt and black pepper
1/8 teaspoon nutmeg
1½ cups milk
½-inch cubes Velveeta cheese to equal 3 cups

Preheat oven to 350°.

Cook macaroni according to package directions. Rinse and drain well. Set aside.

For cheese sauce, in a large saucepan or skillet, cook onion in butter or margarine until tender but not brown. Stir in salt, pepper, and nutmeg. Add milk all at once. Cook and stir until bubbly. Add cheese cubes. Stir until completely melted.

Fold cooked macaroni into cheese sauce. Transfer to a 2-quart buttered casserole dish. Bake uncovered for 30–40 minutes or until bubbly. Let stand 10 minutes. Serves 4–6.

Lanny's Best Ever S'mores

The ingredients and directions are listed in Chapter 14, "By the Light of the Campfire."

Gracie's Memorable Mustard Sandwiches

1 to 2 slices of bread per person (Gracie prefers classic sourdough or pumpernickel bread.)

Butter or margarine

Prepared yellow mustard

Spread each slice of bread with butter. Then spread with mustard. Put slices together. Eat.

(Of course, you can add a hot dog, hamburger, or sliced deli meat, cheese, lettuce, tomato, and mayo as Moki would. Just don't tell Gracie!)

Ben's Tasty Couscous-Feta Salad

1 cup uncooked couscous
½ teaspoon salt, divided
½ teaspoon black pepper, divided
1 cup boiling water
1 Tablespoon extra-virgin olive oil
3 Tablespoons fresh lemon juice
1 large clove garlic, minced
¼ cup thinly sliced green onions
1 can (15 ounces) chickpeas (garbanzo beans), rinsed and drained
1 large ripe tomato, chopped
1 cup (4 ounces) crumbled feta cheese

Mix couscous, ¼ teaspoon of the salt, and ¼ teaspoon of the pepper in a small bowl. Stir in boiling water. Cover and let stand for 10 minutes or until liquid is absorbed. Fluff with fork. Set aside.

In a medium bowl, combine oil, lemon juice, and garlic. To the oil mixture, add remaining salt and pepper, onions, chickpeas, tomatoes, the cooked couscous, and cheese. Toss gently. Makes 4 servings.

Aunt Maisie's Amazing Potato Salad

2 pounds red or Yukon gold potatoes
1 teaspoon salt for boiling the potatoes
8 eggs
1 small red or Vidalia onion, minced
2 stalks celery, thinly sliced
5 large radishes, thinly sliced and quartered
1½ cups mayonnaise
¼ cup prepared yellow mustard
2 teaspoons apple cider vinegar
1 Tablespoon cream or milk
1 teaspoon salt
1 teaspoon black pepper
½ teaspoon paprika
2 teaspoon fresh dill
1 teaspoon Worcestershire sauce
Parsley and paprika for garnish
2-3 sliced hard-boiled eggs for garnish

Boil whole, unpared potatoes with first 1 teaspoon salt for 15–20 minutes or until done. Check for doneness by piercing with a fork. Add cold water to a large bowl filled with ice. Drain the potatoes and add to the ice bath. Once cool, peel potatoes by carefully pinching the skin and pulling it away. Chop potatoes into bite-sized chunks. Then add to a large bowl.

To hard-boil eggs, place eggs in a saucepan. Cover with cold water. Bring to a boil and immediately remove from heat. Cover and let eggs stand in hot water for 12–13 minutes. Remove from hot water. Rinse with cold water. Cool and peel. Slice into quarters and add to potatoes.

Add onion, celery, and radishes to potatoes and eggs mixture. Toss lightly to combine.

Combine mayonnaise, mustard, vinegar, cream, and the next five ingredients through Worcestershire sauce. Pour over egg and potato mixture. Stir gently to coat all pieces well.

If possible, chill overnight to bring out the flavors. Garnish with fresh chopped parsley, extra paprika, and the additional sliced eggs if desired. Serves 12.

Uncle Rocky's Famous
Chocolate Chip–Pumpkin Bread

3 & 1/3 cups all-purpose flour
2 teaspoons baking soda
1½ teaspoons salt
1 teaspoon cinnamon
1 teaspoon nutmeg
3 cups granulated sugar
1 cup vegetable oil
4 eggs
2 cups canned pumpkin
1½ cups chopped nuts (optional)
1 package (11.5 ounces) semi-sweet or milk chocolate chips (not dark)

Preheat oven to 350°. Grease and flour bottoms and sides of two 9 x 5 x 3-inch loaf pans.

In a large mixing bowl, whisk together flour and next five dry ingredients through sugar.

Make a well in the center and add the remaining ingredients through chocolate chips.

Mix well and divide batter evenly into the two prepared loaf pans.

Bake at 350° for 60–70 minutes. Insert knife in center to test for doneness at 60 minutes.

Cool in pans on wire rack for 15–20 minutes. Turn out onto serving plates.

Can be served warm or cold. Refrigerate leftovers. Makes 2 large loaves.

Mr. Mayfield and Lionel's
Delicious Cowboy Beans

1 pound bacon
2 pounds ground beef or ground turkey
1 medium onion, chopped
1 cup ketchup
2 teaspoons chili powder (optional)
½ cup packed brown sugar
1 (55 ounce) can baked beans
2 (15 ounce) cans Great Northern beans
1 (15 ounce) can pinto beans
1 (15 ounce) can pork and beans

Place bacon in a large skillet. Cook over medium-high heat, turning occasionally, until evenly browned and crispy, 10 to 12 minutes. Drain bacon slices on paper towels and crumble when cool enough to handle.

At the same time in another skillet, cook and stir ground beef or ground turkey until browned and crumbly, 5 to 7 minutes. Drain and discard grease from both skillets.

Place crumbled bacon, browned beef or turkey, onion, ketchup, chili powder, and brown sugar in a slow cooker. Mix well.

Add baked beans, Great Northern beans, pinto beans, and pork and beans. Mix well.

Cook on low heat for 4 hours, stirring often.

Serves 12.

Mrs. Mayfield and Catherine's
Delectable Cowgirl Cookies

2 cups all-purpose flour
1 teaspoon baking powder
1 teaspoon baking soda
½ teaspoon salt
1 teaspoon ground cinnamon
1 cup butter, softened
1 cup granulated sugar
1 cup packed brown sugar
2 eggs at room temperature
1 teaspoon vanilla extract
2 cups rolled oats
1 cup semisweet chocolate chips or butterscotch chips
½ cup sweetened flake coconut
1 cup chopped pecans or walnuts (optional)

Preheat oven to 350°F. Cover bottom of baking sheets with parchment paper.

Sift together flour, baking powder, baking soda, salt, and cinnamon. Set aside.

In a large bowl, cream together butter and both sugars until light and fluffy. Beat in eggs one at a time. Then, stir in vanilla. Gradually stir in the sifted ingredients.

Stir in rolled oats, chocolate chips or butterscotch chips, coconut, and nuts.

Drop by rounded teaspoons onto the prepared baking sheets. Bake for 8–10 minutes.

Allow cookies to cool on baking sheets for 5–10 minutes.

Then, remove and cool completely. Makes 4–5 dozen cookies.

Sources: *The above recipes were created and adapted by the author and her family.*

A Note About T.H.I.N.K.

In Chapter One, Mrs. Mayfield used the acronym, "T.H.I.N.K." She then mentioned what each letter stands for: *True, Helpful, Inspiring, Necessary, and Kind.*

According to The Coaching Tools Company, the acronym was supposedly created by an unknown source to help children and adults be kinder on social media by reducing cyberbullying. According to the company's website, it can also be applied to smooth out everyday, face-to-face conversations.

A comment on the company's website, however, reports that some believe the idea behind the acronym predates the internet, having been originally created by Herbert J. Taylor (1893–1978), a Rotarian, in 1932, and called, "A Four-Way Test." The four components of the test are: "Is what you are about to say 1) True, 2) Fair, 3) Used for Good Will and Friendship Building, and 4) Beneficial to All Concerned?"

In my research, I could not find the originator of T.H.I.N.K. People on various websites (see below) use the term without crediting a source. As a former teacher, I know that other educators and I used the acronym with our classroom students for many years.

For T.H.I.N.K., please note that in my story, I used one meaning of "I," namely, "Is it Inspiring?" Sometimes, "I" is also listed as, "Does it Improve on the Silence?" or "Is it Important?"

For more information on T.H.I.N.K., the Four-Way Test, and other communication tools, please visit: people-equation.com, inc.com, rotary5630.org, talinorfali.wordpress.com, acronymfinder.com, and thecoachingtoolscompany.com.

Sources: *The above information was paraphrased from and fact-checked using the six websites listed above.*

About the Author

Laurens Antoine Photography

Sherrill Joseph will be forever inspired by her beautiful students in the San Diego public schools where she taught for thirty-five years before retiring and becoming a published author.

The author has peopled and themed her mysteries with characters after her own responsible, role-model students, of various abilities, disabilities, races, cultures, and interests. She strongly believes that children need to find themselves and others unlike themselves in books if all are to become accepting, anti-racist world citizens.

Her gift of lexical-gustatory synesthesia enables her to bring richer imagination to her writing.

Sherrill is the recipient of two Gold Awards from Mom's Choice Book Awards, a Gold Award from Moonbeam Children's Book Awards, three awards from Story Monsters Approved, and numerous other children's book awards. She is a member of SCBWI, the Authors Guild, and Blackbird Writers. Watch for many more adventures with the Botanic Hill Detectives!

Connect With the Author

CONNECT WITH SHERRILL AND HER BOOKS AT

SHERRILLJOSEPH.COM

AND

ON TWITTER **@MYSTERYAUTHOR7**

ON INSTAGRAM **@SHERRILLJOSEPHAUTHOR**

ON FACEBOOK **@BHDMYSTERIESAUTHOR**

SUBSCRIBE TO HER MONTHLY NEWSLETTER AT

bit.ly/3dx6L9J

THANK YOU, DEAR READERS!
PLEASE KEEP IN TOUCH.

Made in the USA
Columbia, SC
28 October 2021

47983346R00145